DRAGO GELT

THE GEM OF NOVAIO

The adventure

NOVEL

INDEX:

Prelude

Novaio, a strange yet familiar world.

A place where huge birds of prey fly through the air. Where dragons live in caves, high above majestic cliffs.

It's a world littered with ruins from times long past. Some have witnessed great battles. Others have simply been forgotten.

But there are also areas that are inhabited. From small villages to mighty cities, sprawling with life.

The creatures that inhabit this world are just as mysterious as the world itself. Dwarves, elves, sprites, beasts, monsters, demons of every form, goblins, trolls ... the list goes on and on, not to mention some of the beings who are unknown, even to the inhabitants of this world itself.

Chapter 1

The dangerous road trip

The city of Trumar, one of the biggest cities on the eastern continent Braedy. The inhabitants of this city are dwarves. Their leader is a dwarf baron named Teregon. He is a strong and just leader who is beloved by his people.

The dwarves lead a serene life, they are not wealthy, but have enough to live comfortably. They are manufacturing different weapons and tools, which are necessary for their culture to thrive, but they also trade with different goods or work as adventurers.

Adventurers are people, who earn their living with taking up different tasks and quests. They fight monsters, explore ruins, guard traders on their travels ... there is no task too small, or too big for a proper adventurer.

Two such adventurers were walking through the busy city streets of Trumar, they were the dwarven brothers Erik and Timo. Erik was the elder brother, three years older, to be precise; he wore a brown tunic, blue pants and a strange blue hat. He held an old battle-axe in his right hand.

Timo was smaller, not just compared to his brother, but also compared to other grown up dwarves; he also wore a brown tunic, with dark brown leather armour on his chest. He had a strange, big helmet, with a round comb on the top and had a big battle-axe strapped on his back.

Erik took small and slow steps, so that his little brother could keep up with him.

"So, I heard, you've found a job for us."

Timo responded with a proud tone in his voice, as it was usual for him.

"Indeed I have. It is nothing great, we just have to accompany a wagon to the neighbouring village. Our task says, to protect the passengers from possible danger, like robbers or beasts."

"Sounds easy – Ah, there's the wagon and looks like the folks are already waiting for us."

They walked towards a horse-carriage, where the driver, an old dwarf in brown clothing and a straw hat already waited for them. He greeted the two brothers.

"Erik and Timo, long time no see. Looks like I'll be in need of your assistance again."

Erik and Timo greeted the driver and Erik asked him.

"What village will we be visiting today?"

"Prenkra village on the western outskirts of the forest. Why'd you ask?"

"Oh, just… being curious, that's all."

Timo interrupted him and said to the driver.

"My brother just wanted to make sure, that our destination is not Faltner Ville, that is why."

The driver was curious.

"Why's that?"

"We had sort of a mishap there. Which led to us being banned from there. You see, we were supposed to rid them of a wandering hobgoblin, but…"

"… hey, why do you explain that to him, that's none of his business!", said Erik with an angry voice.

The driver started laughing.

"Oh, you were the ones that beat up the chiefs mother?"

"No… that…. That's not how it was. We didn't know it was her… I mean, that she was the chief's mother.", explained Erik, but Timo interrupted him.

"… What do you mean, we? You were the one that put the sack on her head. When I got there you were already beating on the poor old woman, with a stick."

"It was dark and she looked… well exactly as she looked. Have you seen her? You can't really tell her apart from a goblin or a troll, for crying out loud!"

"But she wore a skirt and she brought us supper."

"I thought, the hobgoblin was trying to infiltrate the village dressed as an old woman! And, by the way, why did you, help me smack her, if you noticed that?"

"That is because she punched me in my nether region… that was not nice."

"Oh, so it's okay to his someone, if you get punched in the ba…"

The driver laughed at them.

"… my gods… ha, ha, ha… you guys are just, oh so precious… ha, ha, ha… no wonder you got banned. Heck if that were my mother, I would have probably tarred and feathered you."

Erik and Timo looked at him seriously and Timo concluded.

"Getting punched in the man-hood, is no laughing matter, my dear sir. Yet it is true, that the whole situation was our fault, and our punishment, was just."

The other passengers listened to them and were either laughing or looking at them in fear or disgust. Especially, two old ladies, who, understandably, didn't want to have any business with such ruffians. The driver stopped laughing and introduced the two brothers to the other passengers.

"These, fine young "lady-killers" are our bodyguards. They will protect us during our trip. Don't be afraid of them. Despite their, eagerness, they are proper adventurers, that know how to handle a dangerous situation."

Timo stepped forward and told the passengers.

"That is correct. We are experienced fighters, so I assure you, that there is no need to be afraid as long as we accompany you. No wolf, goblin, troll or any other beast will dare come close to the wagon, as long as we are with you.

The driver grinned.

"Don't forget them pesky old ladies, they pack quite a punch, right?"

Erik looked at him annoyed.

"Seriously?"

The passengers laughed, and entered the carriage. There were only dwarves among them. Two merchants, two older women with their three grandchildren, a blacksmith and his apprentice and an older man in a green robe with a long beard and a hood on his head. He was the one that stuck out the most among the company, because he held a strange staff with a crystal ball embedded in the tip. Erik looked at him and whispered at Timo.

"You think that's a wizard?"

"I am not sure. I have never seen a real wizard, so it is hard to tell."

"I bet my hat, that he is one."

They climbed on the carriage, the driver took

the reins and the carriage started moving. They drove out of the city gates passing the green meadows outside the city walls and continued their way on the forest road.

Timo sat at the back, together with the other passengers. At first, they were a bit reserved, but after a while, they spoke with him and with each other, as if they were old acquaintances.

Erik sat at the front, together with the driver; they talked, mostly about Erik's various adventures. The driver was laughing all the time, while Erik was embarrassed.

After travelling through the forest the driver noticed, that the horses started to behave strangely. Both of them were getting restless, and they stopped after a few steps. Erik noticed that to, so he asked the driver.

"What's with the horsies?"

The driver looked in to the forest and said.

"I'm not sure. But it can't be anything good. They only do this if… "

The old dwarf in the green robes looked from behind them and said.

"… if a dangerous monster is near."

Erik jumped up.

"Son of a boar! You scared me, man!"

"I'm sorry lad." said the old dwarf and the driver continued.

"It's true. I remember my father telling me, that horses sense dangerous animals. Something similar happened a few years back. I was driving my carriage when suddenly, the horses behaved similar to this and then, a big dire-bear appeared in front of us. Luckily, we had bodyguards with us. Just like now."

He looked at Erik and Erik nodded. Timo came to the front and said.

"You stay here, we will go investigate our surroundings for any possible danger."

Erik jumped down the carriage and so did Timo. The old dwarf followed them. They looked at him and Timo asked.

"My good sir, what are you doing? It's dangerous to leave the wagon."

The old man held his staff firmly and said.

"There's no way I'll let you two have all the fun. Also the ride was so long, I want to stretch my legs."

Erik said to him angry.

"Listen, old-timer. We appreciate the help, but there's no way, we'll let you come with us. We're here to protect you, not to endanger you."

The old dwarf smiled and walked towards the nearby bushes.

"Someone's got to make sure, that you don't hit any old ladies, wandering the forest, he, he…"

Timo ran after him, Erik looked back at the wagon and said.

"Turn the wagon around and wait for us! If we don't return in half an hour, you ride back to Trumar, as fast as you can!"

The driver turned the carriage and said to him.

"Stay safe boys. If you won't return, I'll get help."

Erik called after Timo and the old dwarf. They waited for him and then they continued to walk through the bushes. The old dwarf was leading them; behind him were Erik and Timo, with their axes in hands. Ready to battle, whatever might come.

"Roaaaaarrr!", a loud roar echoed through the forest. Erik was startled.

"What was that?"

"That's not a bunny, of that I'm sure.", said the old dwarf and continued to walk towards the roaring.

Timo followed right behind him.

"Sir, you sound, as if you know, what beast it is? Would you mind telling us?"

"Sure lad. That horrifying sound, which you just witnessed belongs to a horned dragon."

"A horned dragon? That is impossible. These beasts do not live in the forest. They live high up in the mountains, to the north."

"Trust me, lad. There's no mistaking it. We got ourselves a horned dragon. He must be one of them wandering types. It's not uncommon for these beasts to try and expand their territory. Heck. There's so many animals in this forest, it's a miracle, that there's only one stray dragon here, with that much food available."

They ran through the bushes, towards the direction, from which the roar came and arrived at a small clearing, where they saw the horned dragon ready to pounce on a deer.

Horned dragons are dangerous beasts, which should not be underestimated. They grow up to 2 meters tall and are 6 meters long. They have a long snout and a mouth that is filled with big, sharp teeth. Their whole body is covered in light brown scales and on the top of their head, right between their eyes is a large horn that is curved towards their nose, like a hook.

The old dwarf, Erik, and Timo stood at the edge of the clearing. The old man said.

"Well, if this isn't a pleasant surprise. Looks like, we found the bloke."

Timo was baffled.

"You were right sir, it truly is a horned dragon."

Erik didn't care much for what they were talking about, he was a man of action.

"Don't worry, a beast like that is hardly a challenge for someone like me."

He jumped out of the bushes and walked towards the beast yelling at it. The other two tried to stop him, but it was to late, he was already standing behind the dragon.

"Leave that deer alone, you stinker!"

The horned dragon turned his head, looked at Erik with its big yellow eyes and whipped his tail to the side.

Timo ran towards his brother, he knew what was about to happen and jumped towards Erik throwing him on the ground at just the right time, when the beast's tail swooshed over their heads, missing both of them. Timo did not waste any time and grabbed his brother by his left arm throwing him behind him, so that he would be out of harms way.

The dragon continued to growl at them and turned his body around, to attack them when suddenly...

"Whooosh!"

... A giant ball of fire hit the dragon in the head. The dragon started to roar in pain, but another fireball hit it again and its head became engulfed in flames. The beast started to yell in pain. A third fire ball finished it off then, turning its head to ashes leaving the headless body slumping to the ground. Its tail and claws were twitching for a while, but then they stopped. The horned dragon was dead.

The headless body was smoking from the scorched neck, when Timo and Erik stood up and walked closer to it.

The old dwarf held his staff firmly, walking towards them with a satisfied expression on his face.

"And that, lads, is how you deal with a horned dragon!"

Timo and Erik were standing by the dragon's body, when Erik looked at the neck that was still smoking.

"See, bro, I told you, that the bearded uncle is a wizard."

"Indeed, it would seem that you are a great magician, sir." said Timo looking at the old dwarf.

"Oh, no. My skills are hardly worth mentioning, but thanks to you two, I had enough time to conjure up three fireballs, for which I am very grateful to you lads."

"Oh, well, our contribution to the fight was less than stellar, I was mostly thrown around from one place to the other."

"Sadly, I have to agree with my brother. The only thing we did was crawl under the beasts tail, nothing worth to be mentioning in a bard's song I assume."

"No, no, I don't want to hear that. It was a group effort."

Timo bowed his head and introduced himself.

"I am Timo and this is my brother Erik, we are very thankful for your assistance."

"Nice to meet you lads. My name's Flumm the Green. Highest magician of the third circle of the sorcerer's guild in Dardar."

Erik looked at Flumm and asked.

"So you're not a local?"

"Dardar, that's a great city to the west, on the neighbouring continent of Rolgoria, if I'm not mistaken. You really are far from home, master Flumm!"

"I sure am. I was just on my way home from a pilgrimage, from the Goldwheat Mountains."

Erik and Timo bowed their heads. Erik said.

"We are really, really thankful to you master Flumm."

Erik ran back to the wagon where he told the driver and the others what happened. When Timo and Flumm returned to them, they got back on the wagon and continued their journey. They arrived at the village Prenkra and Erik and Timo said their goodbyes to Flumm and the other passengers.

The driver reported to the village elder, what

has happened to them. The village elder gathered a few men on horses and they decided to follow the driver and the brothers back on the road to Trumar, to get the horned dragon's carcass. Horned dragon's meat is a sought after delicacy. Erik and Timo couldn't bring it back to Trumar so they decided, to sell it to the villagers or Prenkra, which the villagers gladly accepted.

The carriage and the dwarf- horsemen halted at the spot, where they stopped on their way to the village and Erik and Timo lead them to the dragon's remains. The village elder and his men thanked them and payed them hundred silver coins, and so the brothers continued their way back to Trumar. Timo was sitting next to the driver while Erik was holding the bag with the coins. The driver looked at them and smirked.

"You guys, sure are lucky."

Timo wondered.

"Why would that be?"

"Well, you've got hired to do a job for ten silver coins, and now you've got yourselves a hundred coins and ten more coins as soon as we're home."

Erik nodded.

"Yup. Our efforts and courage have finally paid up. Thanks to that wizard and the horned lizard."

They returned to Trumar in the evening, and went straight to bed.

Chapter 2

Unexpected

The next day in Trumar. Erik had been summoned to see baron Teregon in his office. The baron was the one that overlooked the adventurer's quests, so it was only natural, for Erik to report to the baron, after the quest was finished. But he still wondered, why the baron sent for him so early, even tough he knew, that Erik would give him the report. He arrived at the door and opened it, there he saw the baron sitting behind a large table, looking at some parchments and writing something down in to a big book. The baron looked at him angry, he was not pleased, that the boy stepped in to the room, without knocking, but he still offered him to sit down on a chair, that was positioned in front of the desk.

Erik sat down and looked at the baron. The baron didn't seem to pay him any notice until Erik said.

"I heard that you were looking for me? I was about to give you the report today, so there was no need to send for me."

The baron put down his pen and closed the big book. He looked at Erik, with a very serious expression on his face.

"It's not about the report. Well, to be honest, it is, partially, but I called for you at someone else's request."

"Is it the beautiful miller's daughter? Is she finally willing to accept my proposal of marriage? … Wait, but then … why did she notified you?"

"No, it's Betruvia the seer. She was persistent to talk to you as soon as possible."

"Betruvia, the old cross-eyed granny? But I don't want to marry her. She's hardly considered to be eye candy, not to mention, that she's probably more than a thousand years old. I mean, don't get me wrong, she was probably quite the looker in her younger days, but that age gap is just to much."

"No you dimwit! She doesn't want to marry you, she wants to talk to you about something, so she asked me, to summon you here."

Suddenly, the door opened and a small, old woman stepped in. She wore a light brown robe and had a hood on her head. It was Betruvia, the seer. The religious leader of the dwarves of Trumar, and a respected person in her right. She walked towards Erik, slapped him on the back of his head and said.

"You couldn't even afford to date me. Back in my days, I was courted by many fine young dwarves and even some elven lords had set their eyes on me, but… alas, it was not meant to be, for I was chosen by the gods to speak their will – anyhow, the last time I came out of my house was 300 years ago during the great forest goblin invasion. It was a real slaughter, I'll tell you. We only ate tree bark and cherry blossoms for seven months. My Gods, it was awful."

Erik and the baron looked at her with a

wondrous look on their faces, not knowing, what exactly she was talking about. Betruvia noticed that and continued.

"Erik! Is it true that you helped a stranger whack a horned dragon?"

"Yes, but, just to be clear, the stranger helped us. I admit that he was the one killing it, but only after we softened the beast up for him."

"Fiddlesticks! These are unimportant details. You encountered a horned dragon in the forest, wanted to slay it, but in return you were rescued by a stranger, who finished the beast off, instead of you. That's how it happened!"

"Easy there, lady! You make me look like a total wuss in front of the baron."

"Who cares about your image? Listen! It was 123 years ago that I got the vision of this happening. It was a very clear vision, it was almost, as if I was there myself. I rarely get such clear visions, so I asked the gods what to do if the situation arose."

The baron asked her.

"What did the gods tell you? What must we do with him?"

"I'd fancy a reward. Nothing big, maybe my own fiefdom and some servants… or money, money is always good."

"The gods answer was clear. You shall be banished and follow the stranger that helped you!"

"Banished? But the boy didn't do anything wrong. What are the gods thinking? They usually reward one for farting after a snack, and now this."

"Yes, I agree, tell the Gods to reward me properly. Or I'll think twice before I pray to them again."

"That is not how our religion works! You shouldn't question the will of the gods, this event will help you, young Erik, to find your destiny. You are hardly considered to be a great warrior, nor will you ever accomplish any great deed in our city. Your future lies far away. So say the gods!"

"Sounds more like the gods are insulting me. - So I have to follow the bearded uncle and then what?"

"I don't know. That's all the gods would tell me."

"Shit, when they handed out religions, we dwarves got the short end of the stick. Right? – What happens if I don't follow the gods orders?"

Betruvias face turned pale, she looked at him with a frightened expression on her face and said.

"Rats! Big, fat rats! Gnawing the flesh from our bones. Rats!"

"I'll be on my way then. Bye, bye."

§

So it was decided, that Erik would leave the city and follow Flumm to Rolgoria. He was not really happy about it, but he was not brave enough, to stand against the decision of the gods. He was packing his belongings in to a bag when suddenly someone knocked on his door.

"Come in bro, it's not locked."

Timo stepped in and wondered.

"How did you know it was me?"

"Because you're the only one who knocks. But you shouldn't have bothered to come here, I'd have come to say goodbye to you anyway."

"So you are really going to leave us?"

"Betruvia said that if I didn't, the gods would punish me and everyone in this city with a plague of giant rats."

"That sounds disturbing."

"As was the look on her face, when she told me that. - So I thought now would be a good time for me to go out in to the world. You know, turn a new leaf in the book of my life, as the bards say.

"I see. Then I have no other choice but to join you."

"What, but Betruvia said that "I" was destined to follow the wizard."

"Betruvia told you that, but she didn't mention

anything about you going alone. You are my brother, my best friend and the only family, that I got. It goes without saying that I will accompany you!"

Erik walked towards his little brother. He didn't know what to say to him. He thought about all the adventures, that they have been through and his eyes became teary. Timo noticed that and hugged his big brother saying.

"There is no way, that I would let you go alone."

"Thanks little buddy."

Meanwhile Betruvia was in her house standing next to her magical cauldron, watching the two brothers through it. She looked at them and thought to herself.

"I didn't see that coming. And neither were you, gods."

Chapter 3

Every journey starts with a step

So, the two of them took off. They left their home and travelled west. When they reached the end of the forest, they stood before a great desert. Their faces turned pale, in shock. They couldn't believe that they would actually travel this barren land, but there was no way back, so they took the next step and the next one, and so on and so on...

They decided to walk only for a few hours in the morning and then they put up a tent and rested for the day until sundown, after that they continued to walk for a few hours in the evening and rested again. Sometimes they were lucky finding some big rocks that would give them shade. Once they even had the fortune to get to an oasis. But it was still very exhausting. They walked across the desert for several days, until they reached a jungle.

The jungle was a bit easier to pass through. The only thing, that bothered them, were the mosquitoes. They travelled through the jungle during the day, they knew, that the jungle had many dangerous predators, but lucky for them, they were all nocturnal. They looked for a safe hiding place before the night started. The first night, they hid on a big tree. One of them was sleeping while the other one stood guard. The second night, they found a small cave on a cliff, hidden behind some vines. They climbed to the cave and were much safer there, than they were on the tree, the night before, but Timo still guarded them for a few hours until he was sure, that it was safe. Then he also went to sleep. There was no need for them to look for a safe hiding place for the third night, as they have already reached the edge of the jungle.

They crossed a small creek and entered a large plane with tall grass. From a far, they could see a town... no, it was no town, it was a port. They noticed the sound of the seagulls and the splashing of the waves, they finally made it to the farthest western edge of the continent, and they were finally at the port city, Streppa.

After walking through the tall grass, they got to the main road. The road led directly to the city, so they followed it. The first buildings started to appear in front of them. First, there were only smaller houses and a few people here and there, but the closer they got to the port, the more people they started to meet. Erik said to Timo.

"Thank goodness we're back in civilization. It's so nice to walk through a city again, isn't it?"

"Truly, and right on time. Our supplies are almost gone."

"Yeah, what if... wait, look at that a market place over there. It's as large as our hometown."

"So it seems. It would be wise for us to restock on food and beverages before we continue our journey."

"Why? We'll take a ship to Rolgoria, they will

definitely have food on the ship; it's common sense to give food to passenger's right? We can restock as soon as we get to the port there."

"I heard that the food on ships mostly consists of smoked, salty meat, dry bread and fresh water. It would be wise to stock up on some fruits and vegetables, just to be sure."

"But I don't wanna go shopping. It's boring."

"Well then, let us split up. You go to the port and find us a ship and I will go to the market place and get us provisions. What do you say?"

"Now that's more like it!"

Erik gave Timo his bag with coins and ran of to the port. Timo just sighed and walked towards the market place. While Timo was shopping, Erik was walking around the port looking at the ships. Some were leaving, some of them were waiting and some of them were arriving at the port. He looked at the sailors on the ships. The workers transported cargo from or to the ships. It was something he only heard of from travellers that were passing by their home, he never thought, that he would someday get the chance to see all of this. He walked towards a small pier where he could get a better view at the port. He looked at the ships that were still tied down. There were three of them. He knew, that one of these ships would take them to Rolgoria all he had to do was ask.

After a while, Timo got to the port, with one bag on his back and one in his hand. He looked around the port, when he finally spotted Erik. Erik waved with his hands.

"Timo, over here! I've found us a ship!"

Erik was standing in front of a large sailing ship. Next to him was a big dwarf with a bandana on his head, a sleeveless shirt and a bright red skin tone. Timo walked towards them and asked.

"Is it true, are you willing to take us with you?"

"That's right. The name's Dolfenk, I'm the captain of this ship here, the Rosie Red. Your brother, told me, that you were looking for a way to get to Rolgoria. Well, we're currently the only ship sailing there and as luck would have it, there is one cabin left, but only if you have enough money."

"How much would that be?"

"20 silver coins for two people and you'll get some grub. Two meals a day. So, what do you say?"

Timo and Erik looked at each other; Timo counted the coins in his bag and said.

"Lead us to our cabin, captain."

So the two of them sailed towards Rolgoria.

Chapter 4

A dark being

The northern mountains of Rolgoria, a desolate and dark place. Only a few birds could be seen flying through the skies, here and there. The mountains were high and steep; their peaks were almost above the clouds and on one of those peaks lied an old, abandoned fortress.

It was an odd looking structure. It was comprised of two square buildings that were connected to an "L" shape and on the right side was a giant, round tower with a strange looking head on the top. A bizarre grimace with an open mouth with big teeth, a long nose and two eyes, it looked like a giant tikki. In the middle, between the tower and the square buildings, was a staircase that led to the main gate.

From the distance, one could see a small figure approaching the gate of the ancient building. The fortress might have seemed abandoned, but it was not a ruin. No one in his right mind would dare to go near it, much less enter it. But not him, not the small person, who then stood in front of the gate.

It was a strange creature, hardly taller than a goblin. It had light green skin, ears that were shaped like fish fins, a small owl like beak and a pair of evil looking yellow eyes. It wore a dark green robe with strange ornaments on it and it had a green, rat-like tail dragging after it. It was not a goblin, an imp or a troll. No. It was something different. Something evil but also very powerful, despite it's size. It was a demon. The demon raised his right hand and pointed it to the gate, chanting a strange spell. The gate opened up and the demon stepped through the gateway. He looked around and started to talk to himself.

"15 years I've been looking for this damn place. They told me I was crazy, a nut, a naive little runt chasing fairy tales, they even poked me in my tummy with a stick ... that hurt."

He walked in to the building and stood at a great, dark entrance, continuing his monologue.

"... how wrong they were. And my tummy is fine too. I almost have a six-pack. Here I am, in the fortress of Volimir, the first and greatest king of Novaio. At first sight, it seems to be an empty building in an unpleasant state, hardly better than an old ruin or an elven hostel. - Cursed elves and their hard hostel beds and stone bread. Cursed they be - But even ruins can hide secrets and it is hardly different with this old building here. I only hope there's more than one toller. I don't have all day to search for the loo."

He started walking through the hallways that were build of dark grey stone bricks.

"It's a maze of corridors and doors. A floor plan would have been handy. But I'm not worried because I know what I'm looking for and how to find it."

The demon raised his hand again and chanted.

"Tracking- ghost appear!"

A bright light illuminated the hallway and a small shining orb appeared before him. It flickered and swooshed around his palm as if it was waiting for the demons command.

"The tracking- ghost, a common spell that helps you find lost things in a building. But they must be things that the caster possessed before or else it's all for naught... This might be a problem, but it is hardly a problem for an experienced spellcaster such as I. I know how to how to modify this spell, to help me find what I seek. Those numbskulls from the sorcerer's guild underestimated me."

He muttered a spell and the little orb started to move away from him. At first glance, one would think it tried to escape, but that would not be the case. It was leading its caster towards his "lost" item. Toward his goal. The orb lead the demon through the hallway, over a staircase through numerous rooms, until it finally stopped at a door. It swirled in front of it in circles, signalling its master, that it found what he desired.

"Ah, here it is."

The small orb disappeared; the demon opened the door and entered a room that was illuminated by a strange looking gem, which floated on top of a stone pedestal. He reached for the gem with his hand.

"Hidden behind one of the countless doors. According to legend, it's always in a different place. The eye of Volimir ... looks more like a Jewel to me."

He held the jewel in his hand, the light from it changed from white to red. The demon laughed.

"This is it. The first key that unlocks the secrets of this fortress. Although it does look like a jewel."

He looked at the jewel and commanded it.

"Listen, you eye, jewel, thingy, whatever... I've found you, so I order you to reveal your secrets to me! Take me to the throne room!"

Suddenly one of the walls opened up revealing a hidden hallway lightened up by torches on the walls.

"Ah, how nice, and even with lighting and everything. As it befits the future ruler of Novaio."

He walked through the hallway entering a giant room.

"The throne of Volimir, the first king... No, wrong...this is the throne of Vragon the demon king. A bit too big for my taste but a cushion here and a blanket there and it will fit."

Vragon walked towards the giant throne made of stone and sat down on it. Still holding on to the jewel with a tight grip.

"The first eye is here, now I still need the second one. And then I can absorb the power of Volimir - Fortress of Volimir! I command you, show me the location of the second eye!"

But nothing happened.

"Well, that would be too easy. But one can try. Fortunately, I already have someone working on it... I'd better stop talking to myself. People may start thinking that I'm crazy."

Chapter 5

Sailing through the sea

Out on the sea, a few kilometres away from the mainland, was a small raft made from wooden planks, a table and three barrels. It was crudely constructed. The person, who made it, seemed to be in a hurry, to build it, as if he had no other materials to choose from. On the raft lied a small figure - one would mistake it for a dwarf, but after a closer look, it wasn't even similar to a dwarf, except for his height. His body was covered in blue fur, except for his head, which seemed to had dark blue, pointy hair. He wore dark orange pants, with suspenders made of ropes and dirty brown shoes. Through the back of his trousers sticked a short dark blue tail. His face resembled a dog or a wolf, a strange creature indeed. He was covering under a blanket, that he made in to a tent, which protected him from the hot sun. He stepped out from his cover and looked around.

"Sigh, so much water. So damn close but still… Damn! I'm getting farther and farther away from the land. What the heck… argh…!"

He threw himself down on the back and started to flail with his arms and legs like an angry, small child – then he stopped and looked at the sky. The clouds were passing by him, he knew, that he was being carried away from the mainland, by the strong sea-currents. It was hopeless. He was hopeless. He closed his eyes and yelled.

"Son of a …!"

§

After two weeks at sea, Timo and Erik started to get accustomed to their new way of travelling. They sat in their cabin at the table and enjoyed their breakfast.

"Dried meat and water, day in, day out. What more do you want for 20 coins."

"I would wager that you are happy, that I bought us provisions at the port.", said Timo and took a big lump of bread out of his bag and put it on the table.

"Yeah, yeah. You were right and I was wrong. Just wash that smug grin of your face. But still, I... I want pie."

"I am sorry brother, but we ate the last piece two days ago. On another note, have you acquainted any of the other passengers?"

"Sure did. There's that old dwarven couple on their second honeymoon, they showed me wood-carvings of their whole family."

"Oh, that's nice of them."

"And then there's also that band of elves. They're not all that bad. They play evergreens from the time of the fifth civilization. Not really my kind of

34

music, but it's catchy and their lead-singer is a total babe - At least I think it's a she. You never know with them long eared folks."

"Knock, knock..."

Suddenly they heard someone knocking on their door. Erik stood up and walked towards it.

"You just finish your meal, I'll check the door. Maybe it's the elves. I bet they want to play something for us."

Erik opened the door and was surprised to see a familiar face. He invited their guest in.

"Timo and Erik, what a joy to see you again, my lads."

"Mr. Flumm, what a coincidence.", said Timo.

"You were on this ship the whole time? How come we haven't met before?", asked Erik.

"Oh that. That's more or less my fault. I was in my cabin since I came on board. I was meditating to replenish my magical energy. My mind returned from the astral plane this morning so I walked out of the cabin to stretch my legs, when I met the captain on the hallway. We started to chat a little and he told me that there are two dwarven brothers from Trumar here."

"Then you were looking for us?" asked Timo.

"Well... You see, I wasn't supposed to return from the astral plane so soon; I was pulled out of it, it's almost as if something important is about to happen. And then, when I heard, that you two were here, I just assumed, that it might be more than just a coincidence."

They offered him a chair at the table and they started eating and talking, when, all of a sudden, they heard loud yelling coming from the deck. They stopped talking and walked out to see what's going on.

They arrived on the upper deck and saw a sailor and the captain looking at the sea. The sailor said to the captain.

"There's something floating in the water. Looks to me like the remains of a boat."

"Yeah, looks like someone made himself a raft. Probably a castaway."

The others walked to them and saw the captain looking at the figure in the water. Timo asked Flumm.

"A Castaway, but the sea was calm for the last few days?"

"Maybe he was stranded somewhere and built himself a raft to escape his loneliness. Or he was on another ship that was attacked by pirates and he's the only one left."

The sailor called to the captain.

"Captain, it's a kobold."

"A kobold. Well, then, good riddance. No use in saving a kobold."

Timo was shocked to hear that.

"What, why? He needs our help!"

Timo clenched his fists as if he was about to punch the captain, but Flumm stopped him and explained.

"It's pointless, lad. No sailor will ever save a kobold."

"Why is that?"

"Because most kobolds are pirates, and it could be a trap."

"What, if it is not a trap?"

"I hardly think the captain wants to take that chance."

Erik turned to the captain and asked.

"Sorry captain, but would you allow us to rescue the kobold?"

"No way. I'm not letting that thing aboard my Rosie Red."

"How about giving us a small boat? We're not that far away from the coast anymore. I can already spot the land in the distance."

"Humph. Okay. Give me 15 silver coins and I'll give you a boat, but don't you dare come back to the ship with that thing on board!"

"Don't worry, we won't."

Erik turned to Timo and Flumm.

"Alright boys, I've got me a boat, who's coming with me?"

Timo smiled and said.

"You need not ask for my assistance, brother."

Flumm just smirked.

"Just give me a second to get my luggage."

Timo looked over the ship's railing and yelled to the castaway.

"Hello, mister kobold, sir? Can you hear me? We're coming to help you!"

The kobold on the makeshift raft stood up and waved happily with his hands towards them.

"What? What, for real? Man that's great, just hurry up, please!"

Timo, Erik and Flumm got on the small boat and started to paddle towards the kobold, while the ship continued its journey towards the mainland.

Erik looked at the ship getting farther and farther away from them. He started chanting happily, while Timo was rowing.

"Boat-trip! Boat-trip!"

But Timo was worried.

"It is still a long way to the port. Can we really make it in such a small rowing boat?"

Flumm assured him.

"Don't worry, one of the elements that I mastered is water. I'll lead us into a current that will bring us to shore faster."

"Is that possible?"

"It shouldn't be a problem with such a small boat."

After a while, they made it to the raft, where the kobold was already waiting for them impatiently.

"I'm so glad to see you guys. You wouldn't believe how many ships have passed by, but none of them wanted to even halt for me. I thought I was a goner, for sure."

Timo reached his hands to him and pulled him on the boat. The Kobold was really happy to see them.

"Thank you, thank you, thank you guys. I'm Karlo, by the way."

"Nice to meet you, Karlo. My name is Timo; this is master Flumm the Green and my older brother Erik. Do tell us, how did you get here?"

"That's a funny story. You see, I was a guard on a river mill, but I forgot to tie the damn thing down. I didn't know that I was supposed to, so I took a little nap and when I woke up, I was already on the sea. The darn thing was starting to fall apart, because a river mill can't handle the strong ocean currents. Luckily, I was able to tie a couple of planks together and then… then I played the waiting game. – Now that I think about it, this story ain't that funny at all."

"Well it seems that it is fortunate for you, that we came by. Rest assured, that you are safe with us. Now, let us get to the right current so we can get to the port safely. Where do we have to go?"

Flumm closed his eyes and muttered a spell, and then he opened his eyes and pointed with his finger.

"Ten kilometres westwards there is a strong current and with a little luck we will be at the port by noon."

After three hours on sea, they finally arrived at the port of Gran, the first port of the continent of Rolgoria. Timo and Erik were the first to step of the boat. Erik looked around and said to Timo.

"Good thing we have a wizard with us."

"Yes, very fortunate indeed."

Karlo helped Flumm to get of the boat and also lifted some of their luggage from it.

"You guys seem pretty okay, do you mind if I tag along?"

Timo looked at him and answered.

“I do not mind, but do you not want to go back home?”

“Nah, not really. Since I don’t really have a place to call home. I've been living by myself for years. I'm a vagabond. I travel around looking for work so I don't starve.”

“That sounds tragic.”

“Well, yeah… I don't know. I've lived like this since I was little. I was left outside a temple as a cub. I guess my folks didn't want to take care of me. I lived in the temple until I was of age. Then the head-priestess sent me out into the world.”

“Oh, dear. How horrible.”

“No, no. It was actually really convenient for me, since I wanted to see more of the world anyway. They gave me some money and food. I went to the nearest town and started to do all sorts of work. I managed to live this way for two years. Three days ago, I came to the river mill and the miller there, hired me as a helper and guard… well, I’ve already told you how that ended.”

Erik picked up a bag and said to Karlo.

“Don’t worry little buddy. You can come with us, as long as it’s alright with you master Flumm?”

“I see no problem. The more, the merrier. But now that we’re together, where do you intend to travel, now that you’re in Rolgoria, Erik?”

“To the city of Dardar.”

"My home place? Why do you want to go to Dardar?"

"Because of you. You see, our seer told me to follow you. She said my destiny is tied to you in some way, so we just followed you. And since you said that, you come from Dardar, that means, that this is our destination to."

"Hmm. Interesting."

Timo picked up his bag, Karlo picked up Flumm's bag, he said, that he wanted to carry it, since he had no luggage himself and to show his thanks to his rescuers. Flumm thanked him and they walked down the main road, towards the nearby forest.

Flumm and Eric were walking in the front, while Timo and Karlo followed them in the back. They were about the same height, which made them walk at the same pace. Karlo looked around the forest and asked Timo.

"So you guys got banished by your seer?"

"Yes and no. I wasn't the one who was banished, my brother was. But yes, we are here because we heed the will of the gods."

"We kobolds have no such thing. All that maters to us, is to eat, to keep our fur nice and shiny, and to make sure, that the Alpha doesn't see you as a rival."

"The alpha? Is that your chief?"

"Yeah, sorta... He's the guy who leads a

kobold pack. I wanted to join one, once, but then I saw what kind of a authority figures an alpha is, so I've changed my mind. I'm not so stupid like other kobolds, to obey a guy who can bite my head off just because I want a bigger piece of meat. And now it's only me. A lone kobold, fighting against the cruel world, that he's been born in to."

"Until you have joined us, right?"

"Heck yeah… about the food, you'll share it with me right?"

"Naturally – Hearing such a sad story makes me twice as happy being a dwarf. Our leaders do not do that. Bite off heads, how barbaric."

Erik turned around and said to them.

"True, our customs are quite different. We are intimidated by seers and are prepared to change our way of life at the command of gods we have never seen.

Karlo looked at him and answered.

"Well let me tell you something, buddy. Changing your life is better than having your head bitten off."

"I won't argue with that."

Erik turned to Flumm and asked.

"What are you doing in Dardar? I mean your job. What does a magician do?"

"I do many things. I research sorcery and magical artefacts. I test new spells, potions and magical items. I was even an adventurer in my youth, which is why I still help people like you."

"Wow, that sounds great. I wish I could live like that. Wielding magic and testing my proves in combat with other magicians and monsters, like a real bad-ass."

"You're still a young lad. It's understandable; that you have dreams of your future and that is okay. There's no way of telling, what the future holds for you, you know?"

"Can you tell me more about Dardar? What's it like?"

"It's a big city, populated by many different races. Dwarfs, elves, sprites, gnomes…

"… are there any girls, there? You know, attractive ones?"

"There are many suitable ladies."

"Oooh, nice. Tell more…"

Karlo laughed and interrupted them.

"If you'll continue like this, then your destiny will become pretty clear."

"What do you mean?", asked Erik.

"You'll probably get beaten up by a jealous boyfriend, or you'll end up with a bunch of cubs… I mean kids. You guys call them kids right?"

"That won't happen. I'll have you know, that I was pretty popular with the ladies, at my hometown and despite it all, none of them, could keep this stud fenced in."

Timo rolled his eyes and asked Flumm.

"How far is it to Dardar?"

"With a carriage we could get there in a few days, but on foot it would take at least a week."

Chapter 6

Doing well

As the four of them were chatting while walking through the forest, a loud growling interrupted their discussion.

"Hiiiiisss!!"

Erik was startled by the sound.

"What was that?"

Timo took a big mace from his bag.

"Sounds like a beast. A hungry beast."

Flumm readied his staff and pointed with it, at the bushes to their left side.

"The scream came from behind those bushes there. I know this area well, there is a gorge over there, so we should be careful. Follow me!"

Flumm ran at the front and the others followed him. They soon got out of the bushes and stood before a steep gorge. Down there was a strange creature and a figure with a pointy hat. Flumm looked down and prepared his staff, while Timo slid slowly down the gorge, to the creature.

"It's a demon snake!", said Flumm to the others.

The, demon snake, a monster that resembles a

giant snake, with the only difference being two horns on the top of its nose and three tails, that split on the back of his body. The snake moved it's tails in every direction, the figure with the pointy hat hid behind some rocks, to not get hit by the tails. The snake hissed, when Timo finally arrived at the bottom of the gorge. It whipped its three tails towards him, but Timo managed to jump away from them. As it lifted one of the tails, Timo swung his mace and hit the other tail, which was still down. The demon snake hissed louder than before, as if it was screaming. The sound was frightening. Timo swung his mace again and managed to chop of the tail, that he hit before. The snake hissed again and started to flail with its remaining tails and head around in pain. It seemed, as if it couldn't control it's movements anymore. Timo jumped around, to not get hit by the tails and head.

"You want to hit me, do you? It is time I show you how a real dwarf warrior fights!"

Flumm and the others were still watching from the top. Flumm yelled to Timo.

"We'll try to divert its attention. I'll give you a signal and than throw your mace at it's head!"

Flumm told Erik and Karlo to pick up some rocks and throw them at the demon snake's head. The snake turned up and looked at them. It slithered away from Timo and wanted to crawl up the gorge, but it was to steep. Erik and Karlo were still throwing rocks at it. Flumm raised his staff and muttered a spell; a bright light began to shine from the tip of the staff.

"Timo! Now!"

Timo threw his mace and it got stuck on the back of the snake's head, the snake hissed again and turned around, but then a large lightning bolt hit the mace and the monsters head exploded.

The remains of the snake's head were splashing around them. The snake's lower body fell to the ground and only one of its tails was still twitching. Everything was covered in scorched demon snake guts and blood. Erik picked up a huge chunk of the snake's flesh from his head and said to Flumm.

"What is it with you and monster heads? First you incinerate a horned dragon's head and now you blew off a demon snake's noggin."

"What? The head is always the best way to finish off a monster in one fell swoop. That's just basic combat rules."

Karlo, who was covered in snake blood, wiped his face with Flumm's robe.

"S'that so. And why didn't you burn it then, why the lightning, are you trying to look fancy?"

"Because demon snake's scales are impervious to fire, that's why. I needed Timo to throw his mace at the head, so that it would work as a lightning-rod and burn the bloody snake from the inside."

"But it exploded!?", yelled Karlo.

"The result is still the same isn't it?"

Down at the gorge, the figure with the pointy hat came out of its hiding place... or rather, her hiding place, because the person that they saved was a witch. She had light green skin, a purple tunic and a purple pointy hat on her head. She looked very old and had a long nose. She walked around the snake's remains and said to Timo.

"That's one combustible fella. Right?"

Timo rummaged through some of the snakes remains and picked up his mace from them. He wiped it clean with a cloth and answered.

"It would seem so, milady?"

"My name's Willrinna, the protector of the forest. I'm really grateful to you for coming to my rescue. That snake has been terrorizing the area for quite some time."

"I am always ready to help someone in need. Am I correct in assuming that you are a sorceress?"

"Yup. Willrinna the Purple."

Meanwhile the others came down to the gorge. Karlo and Erik were still cleaning themselves up while Flumm walked towards Willrina.

"That's funny, you have the same name as the famous sorceress Willrinna, who fought the scarlet trolls 9000 years ago."

"Funny, why? I am the aforementioned sorceress, you know. It's been a while since I've met anyone in these woods here. You see, I don't like to walk on the busy roads and there aren't many folks who would wander of off them, but since you helped me defeat this big snake here - How about you accompany me to my home?"

Flumm bowed his head.

"Of course we'll walk you home, milady. Come on, lads!"

So they walked out of the gorge through a crack in the stonewall and after a short while, they were back in the forest. Willrina lead them deeper in to the forest, when they finally arrived at an old ruin. It was a bunch of stone pillars, standing around a stone pedestal. The stone bricks were weathered and overgrown with grass and moss. Some of the trees around the pillars have even pushed some pillars and walls down. It looked like a ruin from a time long forgotten. Erik and Flumm looked around, Timo didn't pay much attention to the old structure and Karlo said to Willrina.

"I don't mean to be rude, but your place sucks."

"It is a little … breezy.", concluded Timo.

"I thought Willrinna the Purple lived in a magic castle in the clouds.", said Flumm with a disappointed tone in his voice.

"Right again, my friend, and this is the entrance to my humble abode. I just haven't used it in a while. That's all."

"But this is a ruin?"

"A sorcerer should know that not everything is as it seems. Didn't they teach you that in magic school."

"Uh, yeah, right."

"Look around. We're already here. Come on. I want to show you something."

The five of them were suddenly in a great hall, surrounded by brick walls and two doors in the front and in the back. On their left side were three large stained glass windows through which one could see clouds passing by. Flumm said to Willrina.

"A teleportation spell, impressive."

"Not really. It's more like a wormhole that is tuned up with my life force. I can go anywhere, where that symbol is."

She pointed at the wall over the windows, there was a round stone crest on it, with a red hawk with a long snake tail, chiselled on it. Flumm looked at it and said.

"The red hawk snake, I've seen it once. These crests can be found in several places in the world, until now no one knew their meaning."

"Oh well. I didn't want to traipse all over the place so I left a couple of these here and there to make shopping easier."

"That's just... convenient.", said Flumm with a wondrous look on his face, while the other three giggled behind him.

"Come on, I'll show you something really cool. It's right behind this door."

Karlo crossed his fingers and said to Timo.

"Please let it be cookies."

"Cookies?"

"Well, she's an old granny, so she must have cookies, that's just common sense, you know?"

"I agree. That is a logical statement."

Willrina opened the door in front of them and there was a stone pedestal, with a big gem levitating above it and shining in a bright, blue light. Timo said to Karlo.

"But … cookies look different."

"Indeed. Cookies this ain't."

"It's a gem, a jewel.", said Flumm.

"Here it is. One of the greatest treasures I have, it's... I forgot it. But I know one thing for certain... it's a really good subject for discussion. So what do you think it is? A Jewel? A paperweight? A newfangled backscratcher? It's been around for... whoops"

Suddenly the gem lit up even more and flew towards them, right in to Erik's hand. Erik was startled and the others were none the wiser. Flumm asked Willrina.

"What was that?"

"I don't know. It's never done that before."

Flumm tapped it with his staff and said to Erik.

"It flew right towards you."

"Yeah. Right in to my hand. But why?"

"That's strange, maybe... Wait a minute..."

The gem started to glow in a bright blue light and suddenly it changed it's appearance into a ...

"It's a ball.", said Erik.

The orb intrigued Flumm.

"This... thing turning into an orb can only mean one thing."

"That I'll have to learn how to bowl?"

"No silly. That's no bowling ball, it's a magic orb, a sorcerer's medium. Just like the one I have on my staff. You're a wizard. Erik."

"I thought he was some sort of bard or scribe.", said Karlo.

Erik held the orb in his hand and asked Flumm.

"Wait, are you sure about that? You know, that sounds kind of like a big deal? I always wanted to use magic and stuff and now you tell me that I can?"

"There's only one way to find out."

Willrina clapped her hands together.

"Right. A magic test, but we have to get back to the forest to do it. It would be too dangerous to take a magic test here."

Flumm nodded with his head.

"I agree, let's go."

Karlo looked disappointed.

"Wait what about the cookies!"

Timo patted him on the shoulder and said.

"I don't recall anyone mentioning cookies but you."

"Fiddlesticks!"

They went back to the entrance hall and soon they were back in the old ruin in the forest. Flumm turned to Timo and Karlo.

"You two should stay here, in the ruins. Magic tests are pretty dangerous. Wait for us here."

"We will do as you command, master Flumm, good luck brother!"

"Don't worry, bro, it'll be fine."

Karlo waved them goodbye and said.

"Don't take too long. We got sausages in the

bag, and if you don't hurry, there won't be any left for you."

As Flumm, Erik and Willrina walked away Timo sat down on a stone brick while Karlo collected some twigs, which were around them, for firewood. Soon they had a small campfire burning. Timo poked the twigs in to the fire and said to Karlo.

"I am so proud of my brother, a wizard. What a career move. He could become a teacher, or a healer, or an adventurer... I mean, a better adventurer. I can not be more proud of him."

"Look at you, being all proud and stuff, just like a proper mother, he, he, he…"

§

The other three were walking through the forest, when Erik asked Willrina.

"Why here, why the forest?"

"Because the forest is full of natural energy, which gives a wizard his power. At least, that works for most wizards."

Flumm stops them.

"Here, this is a good place. Now, let's see... first we go through some theory, so listen well, lad! – You see, conjuring is actually not difficult, as soon as you realize that you have the necessary know-how, that is.”

“What know-how?”

“Wizards, sorceresses, witches or any kind of spellcasters, are connected to the four elements, Earth, wind and fire… and air. Every wizard masters at least one element. Experienced spellcasters, like me, can master two elements. Mine are fire and water. Our head wizard, the Magus, controls three elements. Those who are particularly gifted can even combine or bend the elements and thus perform great spells. Like healing, windstorm, regeneration or the lightning strike, that I used on the demon snake. A beginner can use up to two spells a day. But they're not that powerful, usually it's little fireballs, waterballs, or a minor healing.”

“Wait, are you saying a wizard can't do magic all the time? That sucks!”

“More experienced wizards can use up to six spells a day, but if they are big spells the number is halved. So three big spells a day.”

“And me?”

“A beginner like you would be lucky if he could conjure half a big spell and even then you might faint. Magical powers can be renewed daily. So, when you use up your spells, you have to wait for the next day, to cast them again. The better you get, the more spells you can use. But I must warn you, it's a long lasting process or learning. Your stamina and your patience will be tested very hard.”

"Then what's with the orb?"

"Ah, yes, the orb. The magic orb is a medium that a sorcerer uses to focus his magical energy. Some carry it on their staffs, like me. Others transform them into magic weapons, like enchanted swords and shields, but the most experienced of us can do spells without having a medium."

"Like you, when you sniffed the ocean current, you didn't use your staff for that."

"Precisely because I am connected to the water, I can feel the desired ocean current through the sea."

"So you have a staff, butt you don't really need it for your magic. Then why use a staff at al?

I prefer to use my staff when I cast great spells, the orb helps me focusing the spell, and I can also use it as a walking aid or a weapon. Believe me, I can deal some serious bumps with it, if I want to."

Flumm reached out his left hand, muttered a spell and summoned a staff with a round opening on the top, just like the one he had.

"Wow! You conjured up a staff."

"That's no great feat for me - Since you're going to be a wizard, you should have a beginner staff to match your abilities. By the way, the staff itself has no power, it needs a magic orb, and as your luck would have it, you have one right in your hand. Hold it up! Touch the staff with the orb and..."

A bright flash appeared and the orb got embedded into Erik's staff. Flumm nodded, and gave the staff to Erik.

"Here you go lad. Your first wizard-staff. This is proof, that you have magical energy inside you. The orb, that you were holding, is connected to your magical energy. If it wasn't, it wouldn't merge with the staff."

"That's good, right?"

Willrina concurred.

"Sure is boy. It means that you have passed the first step of the test. Congratulations! - Now we just have to figure out which element you have in your blood."

Erik twitched, when Willrina mentioned blood.

"Do I need to be cut for this? Hopefully not, 'cause I'm a heavy bleeder."

Flumm saw, that Erik was distraught, so he calmed him down.

"Of course not, lad. That's just a figure of speech. You just have to raise the staff up, close your eyes and visualize the first element that comes to your mind."

"All right, then. Here we go."

As soon as Timo did that, a giant flame appeared from his staff. Flumm and Willrina were surprised to see that. Flumm was cautions

"Son of a boar! That's one big flame, it would be for the best if we stop the…"

But before he could finish his sentence, the flame exploded.

There they were three figures dirtied with sooth of the flame that Erik conjured. Luckily they weren't harmed, only a bit scorched, nothing that a minor healing spell couldn't fix.

Erik looked at his hands and at the other two and laughed.

"Ha, ha. Holy tooth fairy! What was that?"

Flumm wiped the black sooth from his face and said.

"Obviously, you have mastered two elements, as I have. But in your case it's fire and air."

"How do you know which ones and why did it blow up?"

"You put too much air in the fire so it automatically turned into a fireball and exploded."

"Ha! Take that, physics!"

Meanwhile back in the ruin, Timo and Karlo were grilling sausages over the campfire. Time looked back at the forest.

"Did you hear that?"

"Yeah, and I can smell it, too. Looks like we're not the only ones grilling sausages

Chapter 7

A place to stay for the night

They stayed at Willrinas castle in the clouds for three days. In that time, Flumm and Willrina, were training Erik to control his magic. Willrina was very hospitable to her guests. She said that she didn't have guests for millennia, so she gave them the finest of foods and drinks, that she could muster up. After three days, they decided to continue their journey to Dardar.

Willrina teleported them back to the forest ruins.

"I wish you good luck on your journey and feel free to stop by if you're in the area again. My teleporter is always available for you guys; I tuned it to your magical energy. And keep practicing, boy."

"Will do. Thank you very much Willrinna."

Flumm held his staff in his hands and bowed his head.

"Yes, thank you very much and don't worry, I will take care of the lad."

Karlo and Timo had their bags full with provisions. Karlo poked Timo with his elbow.

"See, I told you that the grandma was gonna give us cookies."

"Yes, yes, and they are truly delicious. Cookies befitting a king."

They waved with their hands at Willrina and she waved them back. They walked through the bushes and soon, they were back on the main road of the forest. Erik had his staff in his right hand and his bag on his left shoulder. He looked at the staff and said.

"Two elements right from the start. I guess that means I'm very talented. If I had been a wizard since childhood, I would have surely skipped a few grades at magic school. Am I right, or am I right?"

Flumm looked at the boy and said with a smile on his face.

"You could be considered a prodigy, but you should be more careful. Your magic is awfully strong for someone as young as you. You have to learn to control it."

"No problem. I'm a prodigy after all. Where to now?"

"To the town of Widonkare."

Karlo looked surprised when, Flumm mentioned Widonkare and asked him.

"Widonkare, but that's not on the way to Dardar. Actually, it's one heck of a detour, if you ask me."

"I know, but this forest is too dangerous to spend the night in, so it would be best if we stopped at an inn and as you can see, we'll be fine here."

They came out of the forest and Flumm

pointed towards a small town. It was small compared to where Timo and Erik lived, but for a frontier town, it was fairly big. There was a tall wall made of logs around the town. One could only spot a few dark roofs and windows from the houses, reaching over the Wall. The main gate had two watchtowers on each side, so that the guards could see if anyone was coming to their town from the forest. The surroundings were just tall grass and a road that lead to the gate. Back to the east of the town, one could see mountains on the horizon.

"We'll spend the night here, and at dawn we'll be on our way."

"Well, if you say so.", said Karlo and they continued to walk down the road towards the gate.

They stopped at the large wooden gate. It was closed. Flumm knocked on the gate and waited for a response.

Timo had his mace in his hand and looked at the watchtowers, which appeared to be empty.

Erik looked at the big gate and asked Flumm.

"That's Weird. The gate is closed, is that customary here? Back home, we have the main gate, always open, during the day."

"It shouldn't be any different here. Maybe it's because of the demon snake, who knows."

A small nook on the gate opened. There was a pair of eyes looking through the nook. The person behind the gate looked at them and asked.

"Who are you, what do you want here?"

Flumm bowed his head and answered.

"Good day sir. We are travellers and we are looking for a place to stay for the night."

"No! I can't let you in! Go away, while you still can!"

"But, but..."

Karlo walked towards the gate and interrupted them.

"What's goin' on here? So, we've been traipsing through the forest just to get such a reception now? I don't think so! You do realize that the only reason we got here in one piece is because my buddy there, with the pot on his head, killed the demon snake, otherwise, we couldn't stand here and let you peep on us - By the way, I have a bag full of delicious cookies, I can't just leave them lying around in the woods. Mice could get to them and nibble them away. Where's the dwarves literal hospitality?"

"But we're gnomes." said the voice behind the gate.

"Like I care. Either you let us in, or I'll tell my two wizard pals here to burn your overgrown fence down!"

Flumm tried to calm Karlo down.

"Now, now, Karlo, we would never do anything like that."

But the voice behind the gate was surprised.

"Wizards? Wait, let me open the gate for you."

Karlo looked with a satisfied expression on his face.

"There you go. That's how you get in to a town."

Timo said to Karlo.

"Were you not too hard on him?"

"To hard? You've got to be kidding me. There's no way I'm leaving my cookies on the forest ground!"

Erik asked Flumm.

"Why are we suddenly welcome?"

"Obviously, because we're wizards. Too bad I didn't introduce us as such from the beginning."

The gate opened up and a small man appeared before them, a gnome. He was hardly taller than Timo; he wore a green shirt with a brown west and had a big white moustache. Around his neck was a golden necklace with a big round gem in the middle. He greeted them and said.

"Forgive my behaviour. I didn't know you were from the sorcerer's guild. Of course, you're welcome. My name is Gromm, I'm the governor of Widonkare. Come in, please. Just walk down the main street to the marketplace. There's our inn where you can stay for the night.”

Erik, Timo and Karlo greeted him and walked down the path that he described. Flumm stopped before Gromm and asked.

“You know what's strange, the fact, that your main gate is closed during the day. If it's because of the demon snake, than I can...”

“... no, no, the demon snake never came out of the forest. There is something much worse there, which we must be aware of. But first, let me lead you to the inn.”

§

A young girl sat in her room combing her long blonde hair in front of a small mirror. She looked in the mirror, put the comb on the table, next to it, and prepared herself for work. She thought, that it would probably, be just another long day at the inn. She was dressed in a yellow skirt and wore a white blouse with a black west over it. Around her waist was a white apron. She heard loud voices coming from outside and ran to the window to see what the commotion was about. There were five people walking towards the inn where she lived, one of them was her father. She walked to the door, looked again in the mirror to see if she was presentable and than, she walked out of the room, down the stairs, to welcome the guests.

66

Gromm opened the door of the inn and invited his guests inside.

"This is my daughter's inn. I gave it to her when I was elected governor. Please sit down at the big table there."

He pointed at a big wooden table that had six chairs around it. Karlo sat down at the end of it, on the left side of him were Timo and Flumm, at the other end of the table, sat Gromm and next to him sat Erik. Karlo looked around the room. It was a big room, with many tables and chairs in it; clearly, it was not just an inn but also a tavern, and it seemed, that it was visited quite regularly. He looked in front of him and there was a big plate with eating utensils. He knew that they would be getting something to eat so he said with a satisfied tone in his voice.

"Okay, me and my bag of cookies are at ease - for now."

Timo looked at him and smiled.

"Thank the gods. Indeed."

Flumm wasn't paying them much attention, he turned to Gromm and asked him.

"Now tell us, what's in the forest that you're so afraid of?"

Gromm looked at Flumm with a worried expression on his face.

"You're lucky you came out of the forest in one piece. You see, for the past few weeks there's been an ogre stalking around the woods."

Erik looked at Gromm and asked.

"An ogre? What's that, some kind of dragon or troll?"

Flumm answered him.

"I forgot, you don't have those in Trumar. You see, ogres are giant's with green skin and long black hair. They are known to be very bloodthirsty. They think of themselves as the descendants of the titans. They may not be the smartest, but they're pretty strong."

"Giants with green skin and black hair? Like orcs then?"

"No, not like orcs, larger than orcs and meaner."

"Son of a boar!"

Gromm continued.

"He's terrorizing all the villages around here. He comes to one of the villages every week. Last week he visited the village in the west. Right after that, we had to erase it from our maps. The surviving villagers fled the forest."

Flumm listened to Gromm and said.

"That sounds like quite the troublemaker."

Erik picked up his staff and said.

"How about we teach this jerk some manners."

Flumm looked at Erik with a concerned expression on his face.

"That is easier said than done, lad. It seems this bloke is especially strong."

Gromm interrupted them.

"Where are my manners, I actually forgot to offer you something. Entiva! Entiva!"

"Coming papa."

A young girls voice could be heard coming from the counter. She walked towards the table and stood next to Gromm. It was a strange looking image, the daughter was twice as tall as her father, the others noticed that, but they didn't want to be rude, so they didn't mentioned it.

Erik looked at her and muttered to himself.

"Oh my!"

"Let me introduce to you my daughter, Entiva."

Karlo looked at the girl and said with a smile on his face.

"Well, if the food is half as good as the service, I should probably consider joining this community then. Hello."

"Greetings." said Timo.

"Good day, young lady." said Flumm.

But Erik stayed silent and just looked at her.

Gromm said.

"Entiva! These are guests from Dardar. I invited them, so be a dear and bring them our best food and beverages."

"Sure thing." she looked at Erik who stuttered something to her.

"He... Hello..."

Karlo interrupted him.

"I'll eat anything, as long as it's meat."

"Right. Meat loafs have the most protein, which is important for the intestines." concurred Timo.

And Flumm agreed with them both.

"Yes, yes, meat is always good."

Erik finally managed to say something to the girl.

"Hello. You got a boyfriend, or something?"

Entiva smiled and blushed.

"Um... No."

Gromm looked at Erik annoyed.

"Hey you, watch it. That's my daughter you're talking to!"

Erik was startled; he looked at Gromm and then at Entiva.

"No... Well, I'm just, well... I, she... you're beautiful."

"Of course she's beautiful. She gets that from her father!" said Gromm angry.

Karlo started laughing.

"Ha, our boy fell for the gnomette. Welcome to puberty. Way to go lover-boy. You're a real smooth-talker."

"Indeed, Young love is a beautiful thing." said Timo and smiled.

Flumm interrupted them and said to Gromm.

"Regarding the ogre - we would be willing to help you."

"What? Are you serious? Well, to be honest, I've been meaning to ask you since I found out you were a wizard. But I can't pay you."

"That shouldn't be a problem, lodging for the night would suffice."

Timo looked at Gromm and said.

"Good sir, my warrior honour prohibits me from not helping someone ... who needs help."

Karlo looked at him all baffled.

"Warrior honour? What's that? We kobolds don't have that, sounds to me like this wouldn't put sausages on our plates. If you now what I'm sayin'?"

Erik concurred.

"I agree with Flumm. It would be enough if you let us spend the night here. And it would be nice if you show me where your daughter's room is."

Gromm looked at Erik with an angry look on his face.

"What?"

Chapter 8

Night talks

After a rich meal, our heroes went to their rooms. Timo and Karlo were walking up the stairs talking to each other.

"I hope there are two beds in the room. I'm not keen on sharing my bed with you."

"Neither am I."

"You know what, buddy. To be honest, I'm not that great of a fighter, I have only fought twice in my life and both times I had to visit a healer… What I'm trying to say is… I'm not sure, if I can contribute to the quest that we've been given in any way."

"I do not judge anyone who can not, or does not want to fight."

"You really are a noble fellow, aren't you? You sure you want to take on the ogre? You heard what kind of a guy he is. Aren't you at least a bit afraid of him?"

They arrived on the second floor and Timo opened the door to their room.

"Fear is not in my nature."

"But that chump has wiped a village off the maps. Not just metaphorically speaking. Doesn't that make you a little shaky?"

"I'm not afraid of that ruffian. Let him come. I'll present to him my fists of justice!"

"Wow, you're really hardcore, you know that?"

Flumm and Erik walked behind them and entered the room next to them. Flumm put his staff on one of the beds and asked Erik.

"I don't see no sword, or axe Am I correct in assuming that you want to fight the ogre with magic?"

"Darn tootin'. I'm pretty bad at fighting with weapons, but this magic thing, seems to suit me."

"If you say so. I'm going to take a look around the village, you'd better stay here in your room and practice."

"Aren't you afraid I'll burn the place down?"

"You've done magic twice today, before we came here. So there's no fear about that. Your control over your elements has improved, but you should still keep working on your focus."

"All right, breathing exercises and focusing then."

Flumm picked up his staff and walked to the door.

"I meant, you should focus on magic and not on girls."

"I have no idea what you're talking about."

"Yeah, right."

Flumm closed the door and walked down the stairs.

§

Back at the fortress of Volimir, we see the demon-lord Vragon, still sitting on his throne, with the eye of Volimir levitating in front of him.

"Boring!!! - This is crap! No matter how hard I try, this eye-gem won't reveal all the secrets of the fortress to me. Looks like, the second eye must be found after all. This castle has more secrets than my mother-in-law. If I am to become the undisputed ruler, I must know them all. Otherwise, it was all a waste of time. I don't want to be pricked in the stomach again."

He stepped down his throne and walked through the fortress for a while. Then he stood before a door, he opened it and behind it was a room with a crystal ball on a pedestal.

"Fortunately I don't have to do everything alone."

He waved his hands and the crystal ball started to shine, after a while, the face of an unknown figure appeared in it.

"Tantoise, you idiot, come in!"

"Yes, my Lord." said the person in the ball. It was Tantoise, the ogre. Lord Vragon's right hand man and muscle.

Tantoise was standing in front of a similar crystal ball, as Vragon. He was in a throne room, inside a ruin in the forest next to Widonkare.

He was big and strong. He had long black hair, green skin and wore a brown robe and dirty grey armour on his chest. Vragon looked at him through the orb and said.

"So…?"

"…My Lord?"

"Don't give me that! How's the search going?"

"Ooh, yes, right. The search. I've searched most of the forest and nearby villages. But you must understand that it's quite a large area and you haven't given me an exact location."

"I don't want to hear any excuses! I've occupied the fortress, it's important that you find the second eye of Volimir! Do you understand? The well being of my belly region depends on it!"

"Your belly… I mean… Yes my Lord!"

Vragon's face on the orb disappeared; Tantoise clenched his fist and said to himself.

"That rotten little devil. How dare he boss me around, me, Tantoise, a direct descendant of the mighty titans. - If only he wasn't so powerful."

He walked away from the orb and looked through the window in the direction of Widonkare.

"He can kiss my ass with his eye of wool cap... or, whatever. All I have to do is loot the last village and I'll get that stupid, old Eye of wollpertinger. Gods, I'm so clever."

Tantoise was smiling to himself. He knew that the eye was hidden in a goblin, infested cave in the forest. He just didn't get it because he wanted to pillage the nearby villages in the area and was stalling his master until he could get to his final goal, the town of Widonkare. He walked out of the old ruin and strolled slowly down the road. He was not in a hurry and enjoyed his night-walk.

§

Meanwhile back in the town of Widonkare. Erik was meditating in his room, when he heard a knock on his door.

"Come in bro."

But it wasn't Timo, it was Entiva. She opened the door and stood by it, looking at Erik.

"I'm sorry, it's me. Am I bothering you?"

"No, no, not at all, I thought you were my brother, I'm just used to him knocking on my door before entering. I'm sorry."

"Ah. I see", she stepped in and said.

"I wanted to introduce myself again, I'm Entiva. I'm the innkeeper."

"Yes, I know... I, I mean. Hello, my name's Erik."

Entiva looked at him and asked him.

"You were probably wondering, right?"

"Wondering? About what?"

"About how tall I am, compared to my papa and everyone else."

"Eh... well, it's probably something hereditary, like blue eyes or ginger hair. I didn't really pay much attention to it."

Entiva got closer to his face, Erik blushed.

"You're not wrong. You see, I'm an half-elf. My mother was an elf."

"Wow! Really?"

"Yup, really. But she doesn't live with us, she lives in the forest of Moonlite. She visits us sometimes, but she's not allowed to be with us and we're not allowed to stay with her. It's an elf-thing I think."

"Stupid elves... I... I mean sorry. I didn't..."

"Don't worry. I'm only half insulted. He, he...", she winked at him with one eye and smiled. Then she looked at his staff.

"Hey, isn't that a magic staff in your hand? Are you a wizard?"

"Well, something like that. More like an apprentice. I've only recently started using magic, but I'm already very good at it, believe me."

"Are you really going to help us get rid of the ogre?"

"We'll try, you see I'm not just a wizard, I'm an adventurer too. I can handle an axe and a sword. Combined with my vast magical power, that should be enough to put that big meanie in his place."

"Wow, that's good to hear, so I can rest easy tonight, knowing that a hero like you is protecting us."

"Oh yeah, sure. I'm a real hero."

"Good evening, oh, I see you have a visitor.", said Timo who just arrived to see his brother, together with Karlo.

"Sup? Oooh, hello there lill' lady. What are you two lovebirds doin' here?"

"Ah, Hello." said Entiva and blushed.

Erik was annoyed.

"I'm sorry for his behaviour, Entiva. These are my little brother Timo and our companion, Karlo. They're pretty good warriors too… ish."

"Really?", asked Entiva and turned around to them.

Karlo just grinned and said.

"Oh yeah, I'm a great shaman, I can even shoot lightning and thunder out of my butt. You just gotta give me enough beans to eat. He, he, he…"

Entiva looked at him and said.

"Wow, I didn't know that was possible."

Erik concurred.

"You shouldn't pay too much attention to him, he tends to exaggerate."

Timo interrupted them and said.

"As for me, I am the finest warrior of my generation. I even have several trophies and medals to prove it. I can handle the sword, axe, hatchet, spiked-mace, bow and arrow, crossbow, ballista, and catapults…"

"… Not to mention eating utensils." Karlo interrupted.

Entiva looked at them with a wondrous expression on her face.

"A magic warrior, a warrior, and a fart shaman sounds like a super combo - Well, I guess I'd better go then. Good night.”

“Yeah, good night.” said Erik.

“You get a good night's sleep, fair maiden.” continued Timo.

“Nighty-night.” concurred Karlo.

Entiva left the room and Karlo closed the door behind her. Timo looked at his brother.

“Do tell, me, dear brother, when did you become a magic wielding warrior, huh?”

“It's kind of true, isn't it?”

“Well, if that is what you say.”

Karlo listened to the two brothers and said to Erik.

“And you said I was the one, who tends o exaggerate?”

Chapter 9

Early in the morning

In the morning, there were a group of gnomes, standing on the marketplace in front of the Inn. Between them was Gromm, their governor. They came to ask him some questions about the strangers, which arrived the day before. One of the townspeople asked.

"Is it true you hired a band of heroes to help us?"

Gromm answered the man.

"They are two wizards and two adventurers from Dardar, they have already defeated the demon snake, that was slithering around the forest and decided, that they would help us with our ogre problem."

A woman asked.

"Where's the catch? Adventurers don't do things for free. Do we have to take a mortgage on our whole town to pay them back?"

"I'm not going to sign a mortgage with the leprechauns of Blornaar, their conditions are the worst.", said an old man and another man concurred.

"Heck yeah. My great-grand-pappy signed one with them and we're still not done paying back the interests…"

Gromm interrupted them.

"… rest assured people. I have struck a good deal with our guests. They only wanted food and lodging for a few nights that's all. I signed a contract with them, so you don't have to worry about anything."

The townspeople started muttering around, they were glad to hear such good news when suddenly…

"BANG!"

A loud noise could be heard, the people got startled, they looked around and saw a boy running towards them.

"It's the ogre. He smashed down the big gate. He's coming over here. Run, run!"

The people started to scream and yell in fear. They ran away from the marketplace. Some ran towards their houses, others ran to the wall and tried to climb it. Gromm tried to calm them down.

"Please, people, calm down."

Tantoise the ogre, arrived at the marketplace, he looked around and punched the wall of a house, next to him. He grabbed one of the gnomes that was hiding in there and pulled him out of the hole that he made. He lifted the poor gnome up, looked at him and asked.

"Where's the governor? Tell him to get here, or I'll bite your head of!"

The poor gnome fainted in fear. Tantoise looked at him. Smelled him and threw him back in to his house.

"Stupid little gnome."

Erik woke up from the noise and ran to the hallway where, Flumm, Timo and Karlo were already waiting.

"What's that noise?"

"Grab your staff, lad! It's time!"

Timo held a sword in his hand.

"Come my brother, the enemy is here!"

Karlo waved his hands in panic.

"The shit's really hitting the windmill-wheel, man!"

Erik returned to his room and grabbed his staff.

"Finally, my time has come. I will shine like the brightest star in the sky."

Outside, Tantoise was still walking around the marketplace punching buildings and trees in the area. While Gromm was hiding behind a barrel."

"Show yourself, governor, I don't have all day! I'm making potato casserole today."

Gromm said to himself.

"My goodness. He's here. What am I going to do?"

Flumm and the others arrived.

"Don't worry, mate. We're already here."

Erik didn't stop, he ran towards the ogre.

"Don't panic, folks. I'm going to show that jerk who's boss."

"Wait Erik, no!", yelled Flumm after him, but it was too late. Erik was already standing in front of the ogre.

Erik and Tantoise, stood face to face. The ogre was bigger than Erik anticipated, and way uglier than he imagined, but he was sure, that he could beat him, now, that he knew magic. He held his staff up and said.

"Hello, I am Erik."

"Um, yes, hello. I am Tantoise the Terrible Esquire."

"Nice to meet you, so Tantoise, I would kindly ask you to leave the good people of this town here, alone."

"What's he doing?" asked Gromm.

"It seems that he wants to negotiate with the ogre.", said Timo.

"What are you doing, you idiot!" yelled Flumm at Erik.

Meanwhile Tantoise looked down at the dwarf boy and sighed. Erik continued to talk to him.

"You know what? I think it's really anti-social of you to beat up the good people here, but I want to give you a chance to leave the village peacefully before I..."

"... Wait. Forgive me for interrupting you - First of all, I'm not here to beat up anybody, but to rob you of your valuables. Second; I think it's rude that you're accusing me of being a bully and third..."

Suddenly, Tantoise smashed with his fist on the ground where Erik was standing. But, Erik was quick enough to dodge it.

"...I can't stand dwarfs!"

Entiva came running out of the inn, towards Flumm and others and asked them.

"What's going on here, where's Erik?"

"What are you doing here, go back inside!" yelled Gromm at her.

"I'll beat you to a pulp dwarf!"

Yelled Tantoise at Erik smashing around with his fists. Luckily, Erik was smaller and faster than the ogre. But the downside to this was, that he could not prepare his fireball, to take Tantoise down, because the ogre wouldn't give him a chance to stop and prepare a spell.

Then Tantoise got hit on the head with a

stone. He stopped punching and turned around.

"Who dares to ruin my haircut!?"

Another small dwarf appeared, waving with his sword at him. It was Timo.

"I'll be your opponent, you monster! Choose your weapon and stand for battle!"

"Come here, you little rat!"

"En garde!"

Tantoise reached out with his hands, to grab Timo, but was hit by a big fireball and thrown to the ground. Flumm stood at Erik's side and yelled at the ogre.

"Leave him alone! I'm warning you, monster!! Or the next fireball will burn a hole in your chest!!!"

Tantoise got up, his skin was burned and he hit his head, but the fireball, was not fatal to him.

"Damn sorcerers!"

Erik finally managed to conjure up a spell and shot a big fireball towards Tantoise.

"Oh, no.", Tantoise reached under his armour and took a small vial out of it, he threw it to the ground and a giant portal appeared before him. Erik's fireball got swallowed up by the portal and Tantoise started laughing.

"Har, har..."

Eric was flabbergasted; he looked at Flumm and asked him.

"What the ever-loving heck is that?"

"It's a portal. But how is that even possible, he's no magician, is he?"

Tantoise turned around, he noticed, Entiva, Karlo and Gromm standing behind him.

Gromm, yelled at the others:

"He's seen us, run away!"

But it was too late, Tantoise jumped to them, grabbed Entiva and pushed the other two away. Entiva started screaming.

"Let me go you jerk!"

"Shut up girlie, you're my hostage now."

"Let her go you bastard!", yelled Erik and wanted to run towards him, but Flumm grabbed him by the arm and pulled him back.

"Are you out of you mind!?"

"But..."

Timo ran towards them.

"But Flumm, the villain has the girl and ..."

"... Be quiet!", said Flumm with an angry voice. The boys stayed silent.

Tantoise carried Entiva in his arm and walked towards the portal.

"You should listen to the grandpa, you chump."

He stepped in to the portal and waved them with his hand.

"Don't you dare follow me, boys!", he walked through it and after that, the portal disappeared.

Flumm and the others ran to Karlo and Gromm. Timo helped Gromm up, while Karlo managed to stand up by himself. Gromm started crying.

"She, she... is gone. He took her. That monster took my little girl!"

Erik started to yell at Flumm.

"Why did you stop us? We could've saved her!"

"I'm sorry, lad. But you couldn't have saved her."

"He's right, my brother."

"You used up your magic for today. But at least we know she's still alive.", said Flumm calmly.

"How do you know that?"

"The ogre is no fool. He knows that as long as he holds her hostage, we can't do anything."

"Then why did he disappear with her? He could have stayed here, if he had the upper hand, couldn't he?"

"He got hit by one of my fireballs, he wasn't able to stay on his feet for much longer. The longer he would be here, the weaker he would have become. He's cunning, he knew that he wouldn't stand a chance against two sorcerers. He had to escape. What bothers me is, that he conjured up a portal from a small vial…"

Karlo looked at Flumm and asked.

"So what now?"

Gromm interrupted them.

"You have to save my daughter, I beg you."

"Don't worry. We'll follow him. I saw where the portal leads to. I saw a castle tower, a ruin."

"A ruin?" asked Timo.

"It's got to be somewhere in the woods, or he wouldn't be walking around on foot, I doubt he has any more of those vials."

Gromm concurred.

"You're right, I saw it to. It's the castle ruin in the forest. I have an old map, that will help you find it."

"But still, I wonder why the beast is lurking in the forest? And how come, that he has such powerful potions?”

Gromm scratched his head.

“I heard it was looking for something. But nobody knows what it is.”

“Perhaps he just wants to expand his territory?” said Timo.

But Flumm wasn’t sure about it.

“I have a feeling there's more to it than that. He didn't seem to be looking for anything specific, here in town. He was just trying to steal valuables, he said so himself.”

Erik held on to his staff tightly and said.

“Let's just go ask him.”

“You're right. There's no point in standing here and discussing.” said Flumm and then they walked back in to the inn.

They sat down at the big table while Gromm was going upstairs to get the map that he mentioned. He came back quickly and spread the map before the others, on the table. He pointed with his finger on it.

“Here it is. That’s the old castle. It’s not really huge and it’s abandoned. It’s in a pretty bad shape, you can hardly miss it, if you follow this path here.”

“Thank you mate - All right boys, listen up! Grab only your weapons, a few provisions and my tent. This castle is pretty far away, so I don’t think, that we can reach it today. We'll travel lightly, so that we can have a quick escape as soon as we rescue the girl."

Chapter 10

Here we go

Half an hour later, they were prepared for departure. Timo and Karlo carried two bags; Timo also had a sword on his back. Flumm had his staff and the map in his pocket and Erik carried a smaller bag on his right shoulder and his staff in his right hand. They walked through the gate in the direction of the ruin.

Erik and Flumm were walking in the front, because Flumm was the one reading the map, while Karlo and Timo were at the back. Erik looked around and said to Flumm.

"Can't wait to kick that ogre's butt."

"Don't be too hasty. We don't know what to expect in the ruins."

"That's easy, there's a big, smelly ogre and a damsel in distress."

"We got a whole day to walk until we get there, we won't make it without resting. There's a small clearing drawn on the map, we could get to it and set up camp, if time will be on our side."

"We have the advantage now, he doesn't know, that we know, where he lives. That jerk will be surprised, believe me."

"I am not afraid of fighting the ogre in a fair fight." said Timo

"I'm not sure, that there will be a fair fight. He did use that vial, who knows what other things he got up his sleeve. What do you think Flumm?"

"We should be cautious. The ogre proved to be a resourceful fellow, he must be working with someone who is familiar with magic."

"Why's that, just because he had that portal potion? He could have bought it or found it somewhere in an old dungeon or a ruin." said Karlo.

"A liquid that creates a portal is not something that can be bought at a random shop. There is lost magic in this world, but it's only called lost, because no one knows, how to use it now, not because we don't know about its existence. This portal potion is one of these magic's. I've read about it in a book, but I've never seen anyone recreate it successfully and an ogre at that, it's just impossible. Ogres aren't capable of wielding magic, much less creating potions. They only rely on their strength."

Erik wondered.

"But this one did. He used the potion, when he was in danger, he even used it, to redirect my fireball, not just as a means to escape."

Flumm scratched his beard and said.

"Well, there are always exceptions. Ogres don't learn by themselves, because they think that they are the strongest and have no need for magic. The only way, that an ogre would learn how to use a magical item would be, if someone else would have thought him."

"Why are we even talking about this? What does it matter to us, how or why an ogre does something or not?" said Karlo.

Flumm turned to Karlo.

"Because if he was taught by someone, then that means, that that person is way stronger than the ogre himself."

"Which means, that we could be facing a greater danger than the ogre himself. Right, master Flumm?" said Timo.

"Exactly. There is no greater danger than the unknown. It's always easier to fight when you know about your opponent. Remember the horned dragon and the demon snake?"

Karlo listened to Flumm and replied.

"I see what you mean. But when you're in a fight, there will always be something, unexpected, that's just how life works. What do we do, if we don't know everything about our opponent?"

"We must use our wits and as stupid as it may sound, we must expect the unexpected." said Flumm.

Karlo looked at Flumm, rolled his eyes and said to him.

"You're right old-timer, that does sound stupid."

Deep in the forest stood and old castle, or rather a castle ruin, made from stone bricks and wood. A structure that surely had seen better days, but it was not abandoned, for it was used as a shelter, by Tantoise the ogre. It must have been a beautiful place, back in its time, probably the home of an elven lord or lady. There were hints of its previous tenants on the walls and in the furniture, which was clearly of elven origin, the few bits that were still there.

The new "Lord" of this castle, Tantoise, walked down one of the derelict hallways. He entered a small staircase and walked down on it, to another long hallway, where there were doors on the right and on the left. Some of the doors were broken while some were still whole and that would be important, for this was the dungeon, and a proper dungeon needs proper doors. He opened one of the doors, there was a girl sitting on a bench, it was Entiva. She was afraid of Tantoise, but she didn't want to show it, so she asked him with an angry voice.

"What do you want?"

He threw down a bucket filled with green-brown slime and said.

"Here's your dinner! Eat it!"

She looked at the bucket and the gross looking slime and said with a disgusted look on her face.

"What is that?"

Tantoise looked at her surprised.

"Potato casserole, obviously."

"Why is an eyeball swimming in it? And did it just blink?"

"Look, if you don't want to eat it, fine. But I'll have you know, that it is quite delicious and that there was no need for me to give you some. But, hey, I thought, I would be a good and proper host and share my meal with you…"

"A proper host? I was kidnapped for crying out loud!"

"No that's not true, you were taken hostage."

"What... What's the difference?!"

"If you were kidnapped, than it would be deliberately, but I didn't do that in your case. You were there, so I took you because, I didn't want to be killed by your sorcerer buddies. I didn't do it because I wanted to, but because it was the best thing to do, at the given situation. So you should be praising me for how smart I am."

Entiva started yelling.

"Praising... praising you? Are you out of your mind?! You're holding me here against my will, lock me in a dark and dirty cell, offer me to eat slime and now you argue with me about semantics… let me out of here! Now!"

"It's not slime, it's potato casserole… You know what… I don't need this. I'm a big, smart, independent ogre in my prime. You can stay in this cell and rot away for all I care."

He took the bucket, splashed the slime on to the wall and threw the bucket in to the corner. Then he walked out of the door and locked it. Entiva stood up and yelled.

"Fine!"

Tantoise unlocked the door, opened it and yelled back at her.

"Fine!" then he closed the door again, locked it and walked away.

"Dang! I hoped he would forget to lock it!"

Entiva stood there while the slime was slithering down the wall. She looked at it and yelled.

"Don't you dare come any closer!"

The slime was afraid of her and slithered back in to the bucket. Entiva laid down on the bench and looked at the ceiling.

Chapter 10

Evil in the night

Erik, Flumm, Karlo, and Timo were still walking through the forest. Karlo stepped carefully through the bushes.

"Damn! Walking through this path is really annoying and slow. It seems like there hasn't been anyone else walking through here in ages, not even animals."

Erik, who was carefully stepping after Flumm, asked.

"Then why don't we use the road, the one, that is on the map?"

Flumm, who was slowly stepping in front of him answered.

"Because, there might be a chance, that we would meet the ogre there. He doesn't use this way, obviously, so it's safer for us."

Karlo who, together with Timo, had it even harder walking this path, because of how small they were, compared to the other two, said to Flumm.

"Wouldn't it be better if we take a rest? It's getting dark you know."

"Just a few steps more. There's the clearing that I've mentioned, right behind those bushes. We will take out my tent and rest there."

"Good idea. I'll light us a campfire."

"No! No, campfire! The ogre could see it."

"But how else are we supposed to stay safe from the local forest critters? I'll have you know, that from my experience, a campfire is the best animal repellent there is. It's also warm and good for frying sausages."

"There's no need for that. My tent will protect us. It's a magical tent, that hides our presence from any living beings. We'll be safe, as long as we stay in it. How else do you think I've survived during my pilgrimage to Braedy."

Karlo looked at Flumm and smiled.

"You have a magical tent? Can you be any more awesome."

Timo concurred.

"Truly, such an object would do us good when Erik and I travelled to Streppa and it would shorten our journey to. – Wait, if you had that with you, why did we not use it, when we were walking through the forest yesterday? Why did we have to go to Widonkare?"

"I wanted to sleep on a proper bed and have a proper meal. That's why.", said Flumm

Erik looked at them concerned.

"No living being can find us in the tent? What about zombies?"

Karlo looked at Erik.

"Seriously? Zombies?

"What, I'm just curious."

Flumm said to Erik.

"There are no zombies in this forest. Now come, we're here, take out the tent!"

They got to the clearing and Timo put up the tent, which they were carrying in one of their bags. He finished it quickly, Karlo walked around it and said.

"This is a magical tent? It looks like an old blanket and it smells as if trolls have made love on it… or with it, not really sure, maybe even both."

Flumm just patted him on the back and said.

"That's what it's supposed to look and smell like. No one would think of stealing such a shabby thing."

"Yeah, I believe you. No one in their right mind would steal this old… orc-diaper."

Karlo wasn't really convinced. He walked around the tent again. Smelled on it and rubbed his nose. Flumm walked in and invited the others.

Timo and Erik did so, but Karlo was still reluctant. He stood in front of the tent for a while.

Sighed and finally stepped in. When he stepped in, he saw that the magical tent looked different from the inside than it seemed from the outside. Not only was it clean and well lit, but also way bigger. There were a bunch of cushions and blankets in one corner, a small table with sitting cushions around it and in the middle of the tent was a small furnace that was already lit. Karlo looked in awe.

"Son of a boar. But how is this even possible?"

"It's magic, lad. Simply magic."

§

Back in the old ruin, Tantoise was sitting in his throne room and moping, when suddenly, the crystal ball, which he used, to talk to his master, started to shine. He stood up and ran to it. The ball stopped shining and the image of Vragon, the demon, appeared in it.

"Where's my eye!"

Tantoise bowed down and said with a frightened voice.

"Forgive me, master. I haven't found the eye… yet."

Vragon's eyes could be seen lighting up through the ball.

"What do you mean, you haven't found it yet, you twit?!"

"That, I... I... I don't have it."

"Am I experiencing some sort of a deja-vu? I could swear that I heard something like that before. I think it was the last time, when I called you... Am I right?"

"Ye…yes."

"NO! No, that is not what I want to hear! Every time I call you, you say that you haven't found it yet! Are you making fun of me? How hard is it for you to find one stinking, little gem?"

"Very hard?"

"How dare you answer my question with another question, you big, green oaf!"

"I'm sorry master... please forgive me. I... I have searched for it the whole day, there's only one spot left in this forest, that I haven't inspected but it was getting dark, so I decided to postpone it till tomorrow. I'm sure, that it must be there."

"You better be, or I'll come over there and zap you with my lightning!"

"That won't be necessary, master. I'll find it."

"Humph. So, be it. Get me that gem and then use that portal-potion and bring it to me!"

"Ehm… about that…"

"What!?"

"Regarding the potion… you see, I must have misplaced it."

"What!?"

"The potion… I've had it in my pocket, but I can's seem to find it anymore."

Suddenly a large lightning bolt came flying out of he crystal ball, hitting Tantoise and throwing him to the wall, scorching him badly. Vragon's face appeared again and he started to yell.

"Are you kidding me? You lost the portal-potion? Do you even know how hard it was to make it? I needed Unicorn tears for it! Unicorn tears! Can you even imagine how hard it is to get those, considering those frickin' horned horses don't even cry. Only once in 700 years they do. Only once…!"

Tantoise got up.

"I'm sorry master. I truly am. But… but…"

"Shush…!"

Tantoise went silent.

"Listen, I'll come to you personally, with my flying ship. I'll be there tomorrow, before sunset and I swear, if you won't await me, with the gem in your hand then…"

"No, don't! I will have the gem!"

"You'd better be."

Vragon's image disappeared from the ball. Tantoise slumped to the ground in despair.

"Damn it! Damn it all! I was so close on getting to plunder that town and now this!

He was angry and started smashing his fists on the floor. Then he stopped. He stood up and walked in to a room nearby. He took a rope and a big club out of it.

"Look's like I'm going to have to visit those goblins… damn it's way sooner than I expected.

He walked out of the throne room in to the dark hallway.

Chapter 11

The prisoner

Flumm was the first to wake up, early in the morning. He crawled down from his cushions, stretched himself and then he woke up the others. They had a short breakfast, much to Karlo's displeasure, since he couldn't have a proper breakfast the day before, but they were in a hurry. They walked out of the tent; Timo took it apart and stored it back in the bag. Then Flumm took out the map and lead them towards the ruin.

They walked for a few hours, when suddenly they heard something. It was huffing and stomping. It seemed, as if someone was approaching them. They readied themselves for battle, but then… the sound started to move away from them. Flumm looked at Karlo and said.

"Go and check out what that is!"

"Why me?"

"You're small and quick. And kobolds are known to be good at sneaking up on someone."

"That is a very racist remark and I take offence to that."

Flumm raised his staff and looked at Karlo angry.

"Just do it!"

"Okay, okay…", said Karlo and ran towards the sound. He was gone for a while. The others were starting to get concerned for him. Flumm said to the other two.

"He sure takes his time. I hope nothing bad happened."

Suddenly Karlo was standing right beside him.

"Oh, now you care."

Flumm jumped up.

"Son of a … where did you come from?"

Karlo grinned.

"We kobolds are known to be good at sneaking up on someone."

"You little… you almost gave me a heart attack."

Erik interrupted them.

"What did you see? What was that huffing and puffing."

"Oh that, that was the ogre. There's a road turn behind those bushes over there. The ogre was running down the road and huffing like crazy. When I got there he already took the turn, I could only see his backside heading away from me, down the road."

"A road?", Flumm took the map from his pocket and looked at it.

"It is. You're right. That's the old road, that leads to the castle ruin. The one that we tried to stay away from."

Erik looked at Flumm and smiled.

"So, that means that we can go to the road and walk directly to the castle. No more traipsing through the greenery."

"I would think so."

Karlo concurred.

"Look, the ogre was running down the road, he was obviously in a hurry, which means, that the castle should be safe to enter now. Right?"

Flumm looked at the others and said.

"It would seem so. But what if he's not alone. What if there's someone else in the castle apart from him and Entiva? His master maybe?"

Erik looked at Flumm and was annoyed.

"What if this? What if that? You worry too much! Luck is obviously on our side today. The ogre is gone and we can walk towards the castle without any hustle. Think positive, man."

"Alright, let's use this situation to our advantage. Come on lads!"

They stepped out of the bushes on to the road and walked towards the ruin. After a few minutes, they were already at the castle. Karlo stopped them before they entered the main gate and said.

"Wait guys, let me check something first."

He walked a few steps towards the entrance and started sniffing around. Erik asked him.

"What are you doing?"

Flumm answered the question, while Karlo was still sniffing around.

"He's using his sense of smell, to see if there are any more ogres or other creatures in the castle."

Karlo stopped with the smelling and smiled.

"I may not be a great fighter, but I can still contribute to this party with some of my talents."

Timo looked at Karlo and asked.

"And what did your nose say?"

"I smelled some rats and pigeons around here. A few bats, bugs and mice, the usual critters that can be found in any old building. Can't really say where they are, but one thing's for sure. There are no more ogres around here."

Erik was happy to hear that, but still…

"What about Entiva? Can you smell her?"

"Sure do, she's somewhere bellow us. There's a faint smell of her in that direction."

Karlo pointed towards the inside of the castle.

Flumm nodded and said.

"Okay lads. This is how we'll do this. Timo and Karlo, you'll take point. Erik and I will watch our back. Karlo, you will sniff for the girl, but Timo should keep his sword drawn in front of you. If any danger should come from the front, you will jump back and let Timo face it. He's proven to be the most capable fighter when it comes to physical attacks."

Timo drew his sword.

"I will keep our scout safe, master Flumm."

Erik readied his staff.

"So we'll be the rear guard?"

Flumm nodded.

"That's right lad. We should step slowly and carefully. Even if there aren't any dangerous beasties around, it still doesn't mean, that there aren't any traps."

So, they walked through the entranceway. There were three hallways, Karlo sniffed and lead them through the left one, with Timo staying close to his side, his sword drawn and pointing in front of Karlo. They stayed in this formation for the whole time. They walked through the old and dirty hallways, past some old pictures, furniture and tapestries. They walked through the building for a while, when they finally reached an old door. It was closed. Flumm stopped them and said.

"Stop it lads! Are you sure she's here, Karlo?"

Karlo tapped his nose with his finger.

"Yup. Can't fool this snooper."

Timo looked concerned.

"We should call for her. Just to be sure."

"Entiva! Are you there?!", yelled Erik, but there was no response coming from behind the door. Erik looked at Karlo and asked.

"Are you really sure she's here?"

"Listen, buddy, I know what I smell and I smell the girl, behind this door there."

Flumm tried to calm Erik down.

"Maybe she's asleep, or she's been gagged, so that she couldn't call for help."

Timo had a grim look on his face.

"Or she's already passed away."

Erik grabbed Timo by the collar of his shirt and lifted him up.

"Don't…. just, don't! That's not cool of you bro!", Timo was surprised, Erik looked at Timo and put him back down to the ground.

"I, I'm sorry."

"No, brother. It is I who should be sorry for thinking and saying something like that to you."

Flumm stepped between them.

"You're both sorry. That is that – Now about the door…"

He turned to Karlo and said.

"… we should take a closer look at the door."

"Yes, we should.", said Karlo.

"It might be locked."

"Yes, it might be locked."

"Or even booby-trapped."

"Yup, you're right. That's the only kind of boobies that I don't like."

"We would need someone to take a look at the door. A thief or a burglar."

"Dude, seriously, why are you looking at me?"

"Aw come on lad. I know that you're a thief. It's written all over your face."

"I… I… I am shocked! Such accusations shall not stand good sir!"

"Karlo!"

"Okay, okay… but how did you figure it out? Is it because I'm a kobold?"

"No, but you see, I have seen many

adventurers that worked as thieves or burglars, I've also worked together with many of them. It was just a hunch, a bluff and ... well, you just admitted it."

"You tricked me, you old fart!"

Erik interrupted them.

"Can we get back to our current predicament?"

Karlo sighed.

"Oh well... Let me take a look."

He walked towards the door and looked at it. It was a big wooden door, with a round knob and a keyhole under it. Karlo looked at it closely. He smelled the knob and the keyhole. He looked through the keyhole again and said.

"Good news, the door is not locked and neither is it booby-trapped, so it's safe to open."

The others looked at him, but they still weren't keen on opening it. Karlo got annoyed; he grabbed the doorknob, pushed and opened it.

"See, it's okay."

Chapter 12

What…?

The door was open, but what they saw, was not what they expected. It was an old bedroom with a broken bed, a table and a broken chair; there was an old dirty rug on the ground a big bookshelf, with various books thrown under it and a chest that was at the end of the bed. But what about…

"… Entiva? Where is she? You said she's here! You said, that your snooper is never wrong!" yelled Erik at Karlo.

"What do you want from me? You asked me, if I could smell her and I smell her. I can smell her al over this place."

"Maybe I should configure your nose with my fist!"

"Bring it on, magic-boy!"

Flumm intervened.

"That's enough! We don't have time for your bloody quarrels! Karlo! Are you sure, that you can smell her?"

"Yes!"

"Okay."

Nevertheless, Erik was still angry.

"Okay? Than pray tell, where the heck is she?"

Flumm bumped him on the head with his staff and said.

"Stop it with your yelling. If Karlo says, that he can smell her here, then I believe him. His nose is better than any detection magic. We must trust him."

Timo interrupted them.

"How about, we inspect this room, maybe she was here, but then she was brought to another location."

Karlo closed his eyes and smelled around the room.

"I smell her everywhere, on the bed, under the bed, by the table, at the shelf, heck even in that chest there.", he pointed at the chest that was at the end of the bed.

Flumm screamed in surprise.

"The chest!"

Karlo looked at him with a wondrous expression.

"What about it?"

Flumm grabbed Karlo by the arm and dragged him to the chest. He pointed with his finger on it.

"Look at it!"

"It's a stinkin' old chest, what about it?"

"Why is it here?"

"Heck if know. Maybe there are some dirty clothes in it."

"But why would it be closed?"

"You think that she's in the chest?"

"You said it yourself, that you can smell her even in there. She's not in the bed, nor under it. She's not under the table or the bookshelf, the only place where she could be is here in this closed chest. It's big enough to have a person in it."

Karlo grabbed the top of the chest and tried to open it, but he couldn't.

"This damn thing's locked!"

Timo grabbed his sword.

"Let me open it."

Flumm stopped him.

"No! Stop that, you could hurt her."

Karlo stepped in and said.

"Looks like it's up to me."

Erik looked at him and said.

"You've already tried to open it."

"That is true. I did try to open it, but I didn't

try to unlock it.”

“So you want to pick the lock?”

Flumm was cautious.

“Good. But be careful, it might be one of those mimic monsters.”

“Mimic monsters?”, asked Erik.

Karlo explained.

“A monster that can shape-shift into simple objects, like rocks, trees or chests.”

Flumm concurred.

“If you touch it, its tongue will immediately catch you and pull you into its gullet. A very dangerous beast, I’ve encountered quite allot of them, when I was exploring old dungeons and mazes.”

Karlo kept looking at the chest and said.

“Nope, it’s no mimic. I know how those smell, I’ve had the pleasure of encountering quite a lot of them, the only thing I can smell is ...”

Erik looked at Karlo.

“What is it? What do you smell?”

“It’s Entiva, but there’s something else, something, that I haven’t noticed before. This chest, it's rigged with a trap.”

Timo asked the worried Karlo.

"Can you deactivate the trap?"

"Looks like a pretty tricky thing to me, but I'll give it a shot."

Karlo pulled out two strange little tools from his pocket.

Flumm was worried.

"Bloody heck! Good thing we didn't smash it, or we would be gone for sure."

Erik asked him.

"Isn't there a spell or something similar we could use to open this box?"

"If it was a magic chest, then maybe, but this chest here looks more like a handmade apparatus to me. Magic could only make it worse."

Karlo fumbled around the lock with his two tools and nodded.

"Right. The only thing that works is years of work experience, on my part."

"How much work experience would that be, lad?"

"Well, it started with ordinary lock picking and slowly but surely I worked my way up until I finally cracked the treasure chamber of Dahrma,"

"Dahrma? The Pirate Kingdom? You stole from the bloody pirate lords? No one has ever done that before!"

Karlo kept fiddling with the lock until finally there was a loud cracking sound,

"Yes, but only, because I was never caught - Voila! No big deal. Way easier than cracking the chastity belt of the troll princess of Gnarland."

"The chastity belt of a bloody troll princess?"

"Oh, it's actually quite a funny story. It was for..."

Suddenly a light came out of the chest and illuminated the room. Our heroes closed their eyes and when they opened them again, a dire-bat stood before them.

Chapter 13

Bat timing

Timo grabbed Karlo by his shoulder and threw him behind him; Erik and Flumm readied their staffs. The dire-bat started flapping with its wings and screamed in a screeching tone. The others held down their ears. Timo tried to hit it, but the bat flew away and smashed in to the door, closing it.

They were trapped now, the dire-bat was flapping with it's wings in front of the door, which was the only way out of the room. Timo jumped up and tried to slash the bat, but the monster screeched again and the sound wave of the screech, threw Timo in to the others. The bat was still flapping before the door. Erik wanted to cast a fireball, but Flumm stopped him.

"No, don't! That won't work on it."

The bat screeched again and this time all of them were pushed back to the wall. Timo threw his sword, but the bat avoided it and started to giggle. Erik was angry.

"What should we do?"

Flumm wanted to answer him but the bat screeched again, this time in another tone. They held down their ears with their hands but it was to late, they were temporarily deaf. Erik looked at Flumm telling him, that he can't hear anything, but it was the same for Flumm and the other two.

The bat looked at them and screeched continuously. Flumm tapped Erik on the shoulder. Erik looked at him and Flumm signalled him something. He pointed at the bat and then he blew in his hand. Erik understood. He concentrated his magic and shot a big gust of wind into the bat. The bat was thrown back in to the door and fell down unconscious. Timo used the opportunity to go grab his sword and stabbed the unconscious dire-bat in the chest, killing it. The bat's body started to glow and then it turned into dust.

Flumm cast a minor healing spell over them and they regained their hearing and were also healed from their injuries. Flumm patted Erik on the shoulder.

"Good work lad. Looks like there's still hope for you."

"Thanks Flumm, but I couldn't do it without your help."

They looked at the bats remains. Flumm poked the dust with his staff when suddenly a loud noise could be heard from behind them.

It was the wall, where the bookshelf was. The brick stones started cracking and moving apart, revealing a hidden path, the shelf itself, fell on the floor. Erik said in surprise.

"There's a hidden entrance."

Karlo looked perplexed.

"Well that didn't happen to me with the troll

princess.”

Timo turned to Flumm and asked him.

“You said it was not a magic chest?”

Flumm looked at the entrance and replied.

“It must have been hidden magic.”

Erik was confused.

“What just happened?“

Karlo answered him.

“I think, I know what's going on. The chest had a mechanical detonator that activated a magic stone inside of it.”

Erik looked at Karlo and asked him,

“What?”

Karlo reached in to the chest and took a small crystal shard out of it.

“The lock here has three detonators. I thought, that I could disarm them one by one, but it looks like it wasn’t that simple. Seems to me, that two detonators activate an explosive charge, but the third activateed this magic stone here. It must have been summoning magic, that’s how the dire-bat got here.”

Flumm nodded.

“Yes, you're right. The bat wasn’t in the chest, but was summoned from somewhere else as part of the trap. It threw us away with its sound wave and then it flew to the door, to cut off our only means of escape. That was quite the experience. Who would've thought, that such tests existed."

Erik and Timo looked at them perplexed, Erik asked Flumm.

"Test? What do you mean, test?"

Flumm stroked his beard and looked at the entrance.

"This here isn't just some random elven ruin. It's an abandoned elven magic testing ground. With traps and everything."

Karlo picked up his bag and said to the others.

"Whatever it is, we can continue our search now. I can smell Entiva down the hall, let's go."

Karlo and Timo took point while Flumm and Erik followed them, just like before. Erik was curious and asked Flumm.

"Testing ground? Why would the elves have such complicated means of testing a wizard?"

"To prepare the wizard apprentices for real life."

"That' one weird way of testing someone."

They continued to walk down the hallway. It was not really difficult for them, it was one continuous hallway with a few turns left and right.

They arrived at a wall, where they saw a small lever poking out of the floor. Karlo looked at the lever and asked Flumm.

"Should I try it?"

"Do you smell something?"

Karlo smelled on the lever and shook his head.

"Nope. No traps or whatsoever."

Karlo pulled the lever and the wall that was in front of them, opened up, revealing another hallway. On one side, there was an exit and on the other side, were a number of doors on each side of the walls. Some were broken, some were whole. They finally came to the dungeon. Erik ran into the hallway and yelled.

"Entiva!? Entiva?! Are you here?"

A girl's voice could be heard coming from behind one of the doors.

"Erik? Erik, is that you?"

They ran towards the door, from where the voice came. Karlo looked at the door, there was a lock, but it was smashed. He couldn't pick it. Flumm said.

"Entiva, stay away from the door!"

He pointed his staff at the door and a giant fireball blasted it away. Entiva came out and as soon as she saw Erik, she hugged him and said.

"You've come to save me. I can't believe it. You really did save me."

Erik was smiling he was happy that she hugged him. Flumm was tapping his staff on the ground and said to Timo and Karlo.

"I would prefer calling it a group effort, but never mind that. Let's get out of here!"

They walked down the hallway and entered the secret passage again. Karlo wondered.

"Why are we taking this way?"

Flumm, who walked next to him, said.

"It's the safest way back and also the only way, that we know. It would be too risky to take another way. Who knows, how many traps are set here."

They walked in the same formation as before; Karlo and Timo at the front and Flumm and Erik at the back. Entiva was between them, so that they could keep an eye on her. They came to the bedroom, where they encountered the dire-bat. Entiva looked at the room and said.

"What a strange place. Where are we?"

Flumm looked at her and answered.

"This is the magical trap room, that almost cost us our lives."

"Magical trap?"

Entiva reached out her hand and touched the chest. Here body started to melt and suddenly the room went dark.

Chapter 14

Request for a quest

Timo opened his eyes. He felt like he just woke up from a long sleep. He looked around and saw his comrades lying on the floor. They weren't in the bedroom anymore. The walls were dark and dirty. There was a small window with bars on one side of the room and a big heavy door on the opposite site of it. They were in a cell.

He shook Erik to wake him up. Erik woke up and looked around.

"Where... Where are we?... Wait, what the heck!? Where are we...?"

Timo also woke up Karlo and Flumm. Erik stood up and looked around in panic. His staff was gone and so were their bags, Timo's sword and Flumm's staff, but not only that...

"Where's Entiva?!"

Karlo looked at him and said.

"The last thing I remember was her melting. Which is strange."

Flumm shook his head.

"She wasn't melting."

"What are you saying pops? I definitely saw her melting away."

"You're wrong, she wasn't melting, because that wasn't Entiva."

"What?"

Suddenly someone was banging on the door, as if he was trying to knock on it.

"Yoo-hoo! Hello my friends it is I. Tantoise.", said the voice behind the door.

Karlo looked at Flumm and asked.

"Who?"

"The ogre."

"Oh, yeah. Right, the ogre... wait the ogre? That mean's we're in trouble right?"

Tantoise was standing behind the door and said to them.

"That you are, my friends. Seems like my slime has caught you."

Flumm interrupted Tantoise.

"I knew it. That wasn't Entiva and she wasn't melting. You had a slime posing as her, just to get us in a trap."

"Off course I did. Do you take me for a fool? I would never leave my precious hostage in the most obvious room in the castle."

Erik started banging at the door.

"Where is she? Tell me right now, or I..."

"... You'll what? Bang on the door until your fists fall off. You can't do anything!"

Flumm walked to the door and asked Tantoise.

"Where is the girl and what do you want from us?"

"I see, gramps is the smart one, he asks the right questions. About the girl, she's not here, she's alive, but she's not in this dungeon. Regarding yourselves, I don't want anything from you."

"You're lying. You want something from us, or else you wouldn't have kept us imprisoned. You know, that we are too dangerous to be kept alive, yet still. Here we are."

"Humph! You really are smart, gramps. It's true, I need you..."

"... to find it."

"... how did... how did you know?"

"I am the smart one after all."

"You're right. I need you to get something for me. Something of great value."

"You're a big, strong ogre, why don't you get it yourself? Why do you need us?"

"You are adventurers, am I right? How about I'll give you a request?"

"Adventurers get paid for their work..."

"I know that. Your payment will be the girl and your freedom. How about it?"

Flumm turned around and whispered to the others.

"What do you say lads?"

Erik was cautious.

"How will we know, that he'll hold his end of the bargain? He's not really trustworthy."

"Listen, this is the only way to get out of this cell without getting in to more trouble. He's got our staffs, our weapons, basically all of our belongings..."

Tantoise interrupted them.

"... Gramps is right, you have no other choice."

Flumm turned to the door."

All right. We'll do it, but we want to see Entiva first!"

"No, no chance. She's my hostage and my only warranty, that you'll return."

"Okay. What's your request?"

"There is a cave in the forest, I'll give you a map, so that you'll find it. You just have to walk in, find the gem and get back."

Karlo interrupted him.

"What, that's it? That's no request? I've been doing milk runs that were more risky than this! Where's the catch?"

"Silence! If it would be that easy, I would've do it myself. The problem is, magical."

Flumm wondered.

"Magical? Can you be more specific?"

"It's... It's something magical. If it wasn't I wouldn't ask you guys for it!"

Flumm knocked on the door and said.

"All right, but we'll need our staffs, our weapons and our bags. We can't do anything without them."

"Good. I'll get you your stuff and the map, but no tricks, you hear?! Oh... I almost forgot, you're time is limited. You have until sundown to bring me the item."

"Sundown?! That... okay, but then, you have to hurry and let us out."

Tantoise walked away. After a while, the door was opened. The slime, the strange creature that posed as Entiva, opened it. He pointed at the ground, there were their staffs, their weapons and their bags. They picked them up quickly and followed the slime to the main gate. There the slime gave Flumm the map. Flumm, looked at the map.

"Until Sundown... Let's see. This is the castle and here's the cave..."

Erik was worried.

"Is it doable?"

"It is, but only if we don't dawdle around. Let's go!"

Flumm started to run down the road and the others followed him. He stopped them after a while and said to Timo and Karlo.

"Timo, take your sword! We'll hide the bags behind the bushes, we'll be faster this way!"

They didn't argue with Flumm, they did as they were told and continued to run towards the cave. After a while, they stepped down from the road. They ran through the bushes and trees, but it wasn't as hard for them as before. It was obvious, that Tantoise had already been here as he made a wide path for them to run through. They came to a clearing and saw a small hill. One side of the hill had a strange opening on it. They walked towards it and stopped right before the entrance. It was a cave, Flumm looked at it and said.

"This is it, we're here."

He spotted strange symbols on the walls of the cave. He did not recognize them at all. He became worried. What would await them in the cave? What dangers will they face? - There was no time for that. They had to hurry up, so they started walking through the cave.

They were walking through the cave for half an hour, when they noticed, that they walked downwards. After a while they saw a dark entrance, they entered it and saw a great cavern expanding before them. They followed the path down the cave, butt suddenly Karlo tripped and fell.

"Son of a … what is that?"

Flumm raised his staff, muttered a spell and the tip of his staff began to shine like a torch. Erik did the same.

"Goblin!", yelled Erik.

Timo drew his sword but Flumm stopped him.

"There's no need for that lad. They're dead."

Around them were more than a hundred dead goblins. Some were on the ground, some on the rocks. Their bodies were everywhere and none of them moved. Flumm looked at one of them.

"They must've been the current tenants of this cave."

Timo looked around.

"That was the ogre's doing."

Erik felt a cold shiver running down his spine. He raised his staff and muttered the same spell, which Flumm did, illuminating the place.

"You said we shouldn't dawdle around. Didn't you? I don't want this to happen to Entiva or any of us. Come on!"

Flumm nodded and they walked away. Their surroundings changed. There were narrow paths that held close to the walls. Bridges, that led them over dark pits. An underground river, that, they had to cross by jumping over slippery rocks. It was dangerous, but also very beautiful. If they had the time, they would probably take a closer look at their surroundings, but the couldn't. They were in a hurry, but they were still vigilant.

At last, they entered another cave; they followed a path that had pointy rocks on both sides, until they've reached a strange structure. It was not a cave or a cavern; it was a building, with a big stone gate, that was already opened. Flumm stopped them.

"This is it. It must be. Looks like the ogre was already here, who else could open such a big and heavy gate."

Erik didn't mind much, he walked past Flumm and said.

"Who cares, let's go in!"

The others followed him; they entered the strange building and saw a familiar sight. A room made of stone bricks and in the middle of it was a small pedestal with a strange looking gem levitating over it. Flumm was baffled.

"What is going on here?"

Erik stopped in front of the pedestal.

"It's... It's the same thing that we've seen at Willrina's place."

"It is."

Erik reached out his hand and wanted to grab the gem, but he couldn't, his fingers went right through it.

Chapter 15

That's a fine mess

Erik tried to grab the gem again and again. Flumm stepped towards him and looked at the object. He turned to Erik and said.

"That won't work, lad. This is a bloody illusion."

"An illusion?"

"Yes. And a very good one at that."

Karlo looked at Flumm and asked.

"And what the heck are we going to do now? We need that thing, right? Or else the girl's a goner."

Timo put his sword back onto his back.

"Indeed. It is of no use for us, if we can not grab it."

Flumm, didn't listen to them. He started to walk around the room looking for something. Erik was devastated; he fell on his knees and said.

"All this for nothing? For an illusion? No wonder that ogre had trouble taking it."

Flumm was still looking around the room, when suddenly...

"Ha! Found it!"

He raised his staffed and illuminated the top part of the wall, where he was standing, showing the others, what he has found. It was a crest, with a red hawk snake on it.

"Let's go visit an old acquaintance."

He tapped the crest with his staff and they were back in Willrina's castle in the clouds. Flumm started calling for her.

"Willrina! Willrina, are you here?"

A door behind them opened and Willrina walked in smiling.

"Well, well, well, if it ain't my dwarven friends and their kobold companion. Didn't expect you guys, to be back so quick. Must've been craving after my delicious cookies..."

Flumm interrupted her.

"I'm sorry Willrina, but we're in a hurry..."

"… and in trouble." concluded Erik.

They explained to her what happened. They told her about the ogre, the gnomes, Entiva and the old ruin. She listened to them and said.

"An ogre searching for a gem? That sure is strange."

Flumm answered her.

"I know, right? Why would an ogre need it. He must be working for someone and that someone needs that gem."

"What is it with those gems?"

"The question is, where's the gem, the one in the cave was just an illusion, and there was the red hawk snake crest there?"

"Oh that? I did that. I found that gem a few thousand years ago. I thought, that the hiding place was too shabby so I've decided to take it with me and hide it in my castle. My castle is a much safer hiding place, than that mouldy old cavern."

Flumm looked at Erik's staff, than he asked Willrina.

"The gem in the cave, is the same one, that you've shown us the first time we were here?"

Erik grabbed his staff and held it tightly to his chest.

"You mean my gem? That stupid ogre is looking for my gem?"

Willrina nodded and pointed at Erik's staff.

"Yes. This is the gem, I found in the cave. I brought it with me and constructed a similar pedestal, as the original in the cave. I noticed it's great magical power, but I didn't know, how to use it. It seemed to have a purpose and when it flew to Erik, I knew, that it was meant to be his."

Flumm sighed.

"But the ogre wants that gem. That was the deal. Are you okay with it, lad? It is your gem after all."

Erik looked at his staff. He grabbed the orb and pulled it from the top. The orb began shining and it turned back in to a gem.

"There's not much to think about. We need to save Entiva."

He took a handkerchief from his pocket and wrapped the gem in to it, than he gave it to Flumm.

"So much for me becoming a proper magician.", he said, with a sad voice.

"What are you talking about lad? The orb didn't made you into a magician."

Erik wondered.

"What... what do you mean by that?"

"Did you forget what I've told you in the forest, when we were testing you? The orb is just a medium that helps you focus your magic. As soon as your magic awakes, you can use any orb for magic."

"Are you sure?"

Flumm raised his staff and tapped with his fingers on the orb on the top.

"Do you think that this was my first orb? You're mistaken. This is my third one. I broke my first orb 50 years ago, then I bought a new one and that one was molten down, by a dragon. This is my third one. You can get magical orbs at any magical shop."

Willrina nodded.

"That's right. If you want one, I can give you one. I have a whole room full of them. Wait here. I'll go snatch one… oh, and there's something else that might come handy."

She turned around and ran away, through the door.

Erik was baffled.

"So I can use any orb in my staff? But I thought, that the gem was special."

Flumm looked at the gem that was wrapped in the handkerchief, then he put it in his pocket.

"I'm sure that this gem is special, there's no doubt about it. But you, lad, are also special. Don't forget that."

Timo interrupted him.

"But, if the gem is special, is it wise, to give it to the ogre? You said it yourself, it is a powerful, magical artefact of unknown origin."

Karlo concluded.

"That's right. Giving this thing to the ogre doesn't seem like a smart move to me. That guy's proven to be a first-degree villain, remember the goblins? There's no way, that he, or whoever he's working for, will use that gem for good."

Flumm, nodded.

"I agree. You are right to be concerned about it, but we need the gem to save Entiva."

Erik said.

"What if we make a fake gem and give that one to him?"

"That's to risky. He could figure it out somehow and what then? We must show him the real gem, for Entiva's sake."

"I know, I want to save Entiva to, but I also agree with Karlo and Timo, that it's to dangerous, to give the gem to the ogre."

"I said, that I will show the gem to the ogre. Not give it to him."

"What do you mean?"

"I'm sure, that the fiend will try to trick us. It will be a gamble, but I'll try to persuade him to let us see Entiva, and when that happens, we'll overpower him."

"How do you plan to do that?"

"... With this." Willrina returned to them with a magic orb in one hand and a small round bottle, with a clear green liquid in the other one.

Timo looked at the bottle and asked.

"What is that? Some sort of potion?"

Willrina gave the orb and the bottle to Flumm. Flumm raised the bottle and shook the liquid.

"You were right, milady. This will come handy. This, my lads, is a surprise for the ogre. Similar to the one, that he gave us, when he used that portal potion... but I'll explain it on the way out."

He gave the magic orb to Erik and conjured up a new staff. They joined the staff with the orb and the orb got embedded into the staff. Then he said to Erik.

"Here you go. Your new staff is ready."

"Should I try it out?"

"No, you should save your spells. It works the same as the previous staff, so there's no need for you to try it!"

He bowed his head to Willrina.

"Thank you, milady. We must take our leave now; we're in a hurry. We were told to bring this gem to the ogre before sundown and it's still a long way to the elven ruin."

"You mean the one in the forest? I can get you closer to it. I can send you to the other portal, the one that we used last time. Check your map, you'll see, that it's just a one hour walk away from the ruin."

Flumm bowed his head again and so did the other three.

"You are a true life saver, Lady Willrina. We'll make sure to repay you, for all, that you've done for us."

Erik concluded.

"About the orb... I'll make sure to pay you back for it, no matter how much it costs."

Willrina smiled and said to the boy.

"There's no need for that, boy. You just go and safe the girl."

They walked back to the teleporter and soon they were back in the forest ruin, from which they first entered Willrinas castle. Flumm took the map and looked at it.

"Aha. I see. That way! Follow me lads!"

They started running through a small path, through the bushes. Soon they were on the main road, which lead to the elven ruin.

Flumm stopped. He took the small bottle with the green liquid out of his pocket and told the others.

"Listen up, lads. I'll tell you what we'll do. First we'll make sure, that the ogre will bring Entiva to us..."

"... but the real one this time. We should be vary of that slime creature, that tricked us before.", interrupted Timo, to which Karlo replied.

"Don't worry, I memorized the smell of that

goop. It won't trick us again."

Flumm nodded.

"Good. I'll give this bottle to you, Karlo..."

"Wait, why? Why me?"

"The ogre's no fool, he'll probably ask us to leave our staffs and the sword, before we come close to him. You weren't carrying any weapons and it seems, that he doesn't perceive you as a threat."

"Okay, okay. I see your point. I'm a bit offended, by that. I am a man after all. But I know what you mean."

Flumm gave the bottle to Karlo. Karlo looked at it.

"So, what's it do?"

"It's a paralysing potion. Listen carefully. When I'll say the words "bloody ogre", you'll take this bottle and throw it under his feet. A magical circle will appear under him, which will paralyse him for 5 minutes. As soon as this happens, I'll cast my lightning spell and blast the ogre into oblivion. Then, we free Entiva, and hurry back to town. What do you say?"

Timo and Erik nodded, but Karlo was sceptical.

"Sounds simple. But, how do you want to cast the spell, without your staff."

Erik answered that.

"He doesn't need his staff. He only uses it as a walking aid and as a weapon. He can cast spells without it."

Flumm concurred.

"That's right and just like you, my furry friend, the ogre, doesn't know that. He only saw me with the staff, so he thinks that I'm harmless without it."

Karlo looked at Flumm, smiled at him and said.

"You cheeky bastard."

Chapter 16

The rescue

They were walking down the road for half an hour. The sun was starting to set, but they weren't afraid, because the ruin was just around the corner. Flumm walked at the front and held the gem, wrapped in the handkerchief in his hands, next to him was Erik, looking at his new staff, anticipating what was about to happen. Timo and Karlo were carrying the bags. They picked them up when they walked past the place where they left them. Flumm said, that they should have them, so that the ogre wouldn't become suspicious of them. Timo held his sword, with a tight grip in his hand. Karlo had his right hand in his pocket. He held tightly to the small bottle, as if he was scared, that he would lose it. As soon as they got close to the gate, he let go of it. So that the ogre wouldn't notice it. They stopped at the entrance and Flumm called for the ogre.

"Tantoise! Tantoise the Terrible! We are back."

Tantoise appeared at one of the windows above them.

"Did you get it?"

"We wouldn't be here, if that weren't the case."

"No tricks, wizard. Leave your stuff at the gate."

Flumm pretended to be startled by that request.

"But, but our belongings won't be safe here. We can't just leave everything here..."

Tantoise reached with his arm to the side and pulled Entiva to the window. She was tied with a rope and her mouth was gagged.

"That's not a request, pops! It's an order! Leave your stuff there."

The others pretended to do so unwillingly even tough, it was all going as they expected.

Tantoise pushed Entiva away from the window. He reached down and threw a rope to them.

"Take that, and bind the other three to that tree there! Then you'll come in!"

"Please, milord Tantoise. There's no need for that. You can't expect me to step before you alone and unarmed. You, as an descendant of the mighty titans, should know that it is not proper etiquette, to make an exchange without an attendant."

Flumm's chosen words flattered Tantoise, he had no idea what the old dwarf was talking about, but he wanted to show his nobility and pride.

"Okay, than you can take the doggy with you. He's harmless anyway."

Flumm bowed his head and Karlo did to. They tied Erik and Timo to a nearby tree and entered the castle. Karlo was nervous, he didn't expect them to be facing the ogre alone. But Flumm wasn't worried. He was sure, that his plan would work as long as he had Karlo with him.

They entered the castle and saw Tantoise standing above the great staircase. He pointed with his hand and said.

"Come here and walk that way, I'll wait for you in my throne room!"

Flumm and Karlo stepped carefully up the stairs and walked towards the direction, that Tantoise told them. They entered the old throne room, but it could hardly be called that. There was an old broken throne, on which Tantoise was sitting, a few stone pillars, most of them were broken. The roof had a big hole right above the throne and on the left side of Tantoise was Entiva lying on some old tapestries. She couldn't move or speak. Flumm and Karlo wanted to walk towards her, but Tantoise warned them.

"On no you don't!", he threw a big rock between them and Entiva. They both stepped back.

"I'm sorry. Milord. We just wanted to make sure, that you weren't tricking us again. Like last time."

"You thought that she was the slime? So that's why you wanted the doggy with you. Ha, ha, ha... you really tricked me. You cunning little dwarf, but that wasn't necessary. She's the real one, he can smell her all he wants."

Karlo stepped towards her and smelled. He looked at Flumm and nodded.

Tantoise grinned.

"See, I told you. Now back to business. Where's the eye?"

"Eye? But weren't you looking for this gem here?", he unwrapped the gem out of the handkerchief and showed it to Tantoise.

Tantoise stood up.

"Eye, gem, stone, jewel... whatever. That's it! Now gimme...!"

Flumm stepped back and hid the gem under his robe.

"Oh no. You'll free the girl first and let her and Karlo walk away, then I'll give you the gem!"

Tantoise was angry, he stepped towards Flumm.

"I will do no such thing! You will give me the eye and then I will smash you and the kobold to a pulp. And take the girl to my master!"

"You bloody ogre!"

Karlo reached in his pocket and threw the small bottle under the ogre. Tantoise was ready to jump at Flumm, when he stopped and froze. He stood before Flumm in an imposing pose, but he couldn't move. Karlo yelled.

"We did it! Now fry this sucker!"

Flumm muttered a spell, sparks started to build up in his hands, he pointed his left hand at the ogre and cast a big lightning bolt at him...

§

… the lightning flew towards the ogre. But then, everything went silent.

The lightning disappeared and Tantoise moved his hand grabbing Flumm by the neck. He raised him up and reached under his robe, taking the gem away from him. Then he threw him out of the window.

Karlo was shocked; he didn't know what happened before he could do anything a big rock came flying towards him, hitting him in the head. He fell on the ground.

Tantoise started laughing. Entiva looked at everything and was shaking in fear. A shadow appeared over Tantoise. He looked up and saw his masters flying ship above him. The demon-lord Vragon, levitated slowly down to the throne room. He looked at Entiva and at the unconscious Karlo. Then he smiled and turned to Tantoise. He grabbed the stone that Tantoise was holding and snatched it away.

"That would be mine!", he said with an evil smile on his face, then he pointed at Entiva and said.

"And that one to!"

"Yes, master."

Entiva was shaking, she tried to fend Tantoise of but she couldn't do anything against the strong ogre. He lifted her up and walked with her towards his master.

"The doggie's still breathing. Hardly, but he's alive."

"Let him! I have the eye, that's all that matters and a small bonus. Come! Let's go!"

Vragon waved his hand and they started levitating up towards the flying ship. There Vragon sat down near a crystal ball, muttered a spell and they flew away from the ruin. Back to the fortress of Volimir.

Chapter 17

Decisions

Erik and Timo looked at the ship, leaving the castle, they twitched around and yelled and screamed, but they couldn't do anything, because they were still bond to the tree. Timo noticed something moving on the treetop near the castle. It was Flumm.

He carefully climbed down from the tree. He was limping from the injuries that he got from being thrown out of the window. He cast minor heal on himself and ran towards the brothers to free them.

He cut the ropes, Erik was screaming in anger.

"What the heck happened? What was that?"

"I don't know lad… It… It didn't work."

He released Erik and Timo from the ropes; Erik jumped up and punched Flumm, who fell down to the ground.

"You said, that it would work! You said, that your plan is fool proof! Where are Entiva and Karlo then? Where are they?"

Flumm was lying on the ground. He was angry, but not at Erik, at himself. He didn't say anything to Erik. The boy tried to punch him again but was held back by Timo.

"Stop it! Damn you, stop it! There's no time for this now! We should go and look after Entiva and Karlo… maybe…"

Flumm stood up and walked towards Erik.

"Listen lad. It didn't work, I screwed up, but punching me won't help you."

Erik looked at the old dwarf. He saw how sad he was. His eyes became teary; he fell down on the ground and started hitting the grass with his fists.

"I know. Damn it! I know!"

Timo grabbed him by the collar and picked him up.

"Entiva and Karlo! Now!", he pushed him away and walked towards the castle. Flumm followed him and shortly after that, Erik came running after them, with his staff in hand. They ran up the stairs in to the throne room.

They saw Karlo lying on the ground and ran towards him. Flumm picked him up, he saw, that the he was still breathing, but the poor kobold was in pain. Erik took his staff and cast a great healing spell on Karlo. After that he fell on his knees. He was exhausted.

Karlo opened his eyes.

"We screwed up, didn't we... ugh..."

He tried to stand up, but couldn't do it. Timo told him to lie still for a bit while Flumm looked at Erik.

"There was... silence. The plan did work, but... something happened."

Karlo looked at them and said.

"It was a little guy. Green, with a beak and funny looking ears. He said something about an eye and then they took Entiva."

Timo looked at Flumm.

"I saw how the ship flew towards the roof. I yelled and screamed, hopping that you would hear us. So did Erik. But we were to far away. That creature cast a bright light and suddenly we saw you flying through the window. I thought you were dead."

Erik looked to the ground, crying. Then he looked at Flumm.

"I'm sorry for punching you."

"Don't worry lad."

"What now?"

Karlo still lied on the ground and grinned.

"Let's go find that jerk... ugh... damn it hurts!"

Flumm walked to the window, from which he was tossed and said.

"We'll save the girl and get that gem back. That's it."

End of part 01

IMPRINT:

The gem of Novaio, The adventure

First published in 2020 by Drago Gelt.

© Copyright 2020 by Drago Gelt, Velika Polana 155/a, 9225 Velika Polana, Slovenia

Editing, proofreading: Metka Gelt

Design and cover: Metka Gelt, Drago Gelt

Contacts: geltdrago@siol.net

ISBN: 9798557423151

Imprint: Independently published

ABOUT THE AUTHOR:

Drago Gelt, born 1982, lives in Slovenia. He is a professor of German language. He is a big fan of fantasy, sci-fi and comedy. His writing is inspired by books, movies, comics and games of different genres. His favourite book genre is fantasy and he tries to involve in his works the influences from all the media, that he encountered in his youth and during his education.